WITHDRAWN

"I have a theory." She crossed her legs. "I think the idea to walk across the lake was Matty's. Matty's crazy, always has been. He's a practical joker, a dare-takClark is kind of a quie   e of them got togeth   us. I'm trying not to   air. I've known these   r as long as I've kno   e a judgment, I would say Matty said, 'Hey, let's walk across the lake to Canada. We may not have another chance for a lot of years.' And I think Clark probably went along with him because it's what Clark always did. But Val isn't stupid, he doesn't take chances, he's a grown-up, not just a big kid that dresses like a man. I don't think Val went with them."

"That's a big theory. Can you back it up?"

"Not with anything hard. But I know my husband. He knew the value of life, the value of our marriage. I don't think he'd take a chance like that."

"That's very interesting," I said. "But where is he if he didn't go with them?"

"That's what I want you to find out. . . ."

By Lee Harris
Published by Fawcett Books:

THE GOOD FRIDAY MURDER
THE YOM KIPPUR MURDER
THE CHRISTENING DAY MURDER
THE ST. PATRICK'S DAY MURDER
THE CHRISTMAS NIGHT MURDER
THE THANKSGIVING DAY MURDER
THE PASSOVER MURDER
THE VALENTINE'S DAY MURDER
THE NEW YEAR'S EVE MURDER
THE LABOR DAY MURDER
THE FATHER'S DAY MURDER
THE MOTHER'S DAY MURDER
THE APRIL FOOLS' DAY MURDER
THE HAPPY BIRTHDAY MURDER

THE VALENTINE'S DAY MURDER

Lee Harris

FAWCETT BOOKS • NEW YORK

A Fawcett Book
Published by The Ballantine Publishing Group
Copyright © 1997 by Lee Harris

www.ballantinebooks.com

Library of Congress Catalog Card Number: 96-96984

ISBN 0-449-14964-1

Manufactured in the United States of America

First Edition: February 1997

10   9   8   7

For Barbara Dicks

Trust not one night's ice.
GEORGE HERBERT

The author wishes to thank
Ana M. Soler; James L. V. Wegman; Richard Burton;
Elliott Shapiro, head librarian at the *Buffalo News*;
and Professor John F. Dobbyn of Villanova University
for their help and expert information.

1

When the phone rang that beautiful spring day, I think I knew before I answered who would be on the other end. Since the beginning of the week, I had been waiting for this call, although I had hoped it would never come.

I picked up the phone. "Hello?"

"Chris?" It was the same female voice that I had first heard in February.

"Yes."

"This is Carlotta French. They've found the bodies."

A chill rippled through me. "I'm so sorry," I said. "Then the worst has happened."

"Not exactly. There was a surprise, a very interesting surprise."

It had been a winter crowded with the kind of troubles that make people come to me for help. A chance involvement in solving a forty-year-old murder two years ago had led to a kind of second career for me, looking into murders when all else has failed or when the proper authorities show a lack of interest or determination. Over Christmas I had worked on one connected with St. Stephen's Convent, the place where I had spent fifteen years of my life before rejoining the secular world. Not

1

long after that, my friend Melanie Gross's uncle asked me to look into the disappearance of his second wife more than a year earlier. And on the heels of that, Mel and her mother presented me with the unsolved murder of a relative sixteen years ago. Enough, I thought, as spring made its welcome appearance and I found out happily that I was newly pregnant. All I wanted to do was get a garden going and watch seeds sprout. But it was not to be. There had been a phone call in mid-February and then a meeting with Carlotta French, and nagging at me all through the rest of the winter into early spring was the feeling that a certain week would come and the phone would ring. As it had just now.

I remember waking up on the fourteenth of February, unaware it was a day that would change my life. I got a hug in bed from Jack, my husband of less than a year, and a murmured, "Happy Valentine's Day, sweetheart." Then I got up and went downstairs to get breakfast ready.

While Valentine's Day is one of the most well-known days in the calendar, to Christians and non-Christians alike, the day is not one of great importance in the Catholic calendar. It's not a Holy Day of Obligation like New Year's Day or All Saints' Day. The Missal says only that St. Valentine was a holy priest of Rome who was martyred under the Emperor Aurelian in 270, and there's nothing special about him in the mass for that day. But as everyone knows, it has become a day on which to proclaim or renew one's love. This was the first Valentine's Day of my married life, and I had a little surprise for Jack that I was saving for his return home, a bottle of cognac that I had been assured was very fine and would be appreciated by a man of taste. I liked that.

It was a little too cold that morning for my sometime

walk, so I stayed inside until Jack left for the Sixty-fifth Precinct in Brooklyn where he is a detective sergeant. He didn't say any more about the day, and I didn't either. Later I would go to a bakery in the next town and pick up a heart-shaped cake for tonight's dessert.

I was just about to leave that afternoon to pick up the cake when the doorbell rang. Assuming it was a neighbor, I pulled the door open to find a young man standing on my doorstep with a long box.

"Mrs. Brooks? Happy Valentine's Day, ma'am. Looks like someone sent you the best."

Flushed and flustered, I took the box inside and pulled it open. The young man had been right. Inside the long, narrow box was a dozen roses, half red, half white.

I stood staring at them as though they were from another planet. Twelve beautiful roses, all for me. I could feel my eyes misting as I pulled out the tiny envelope and removed the card. "For Chris," it read, "From the one who loves you most."

I was absolutely overcome. While the flowers were extraordinary, each with a water-filled tube clamped to the stem, the tiny note with its heartfelt sentiment had left me in tears. Tough guy, I thought. You're sweet as sugar. When did you even have time to order them?

Jack had given me flowers before, but nothing as extravagant as this. I went to the china cabinet that, like most of the contents of the house, I had inherited from my Aunt Meg, and took out her prized Irish crystal vase. I had never used it, but this was the time for a first. I carried it carefully into the kitchen, filled it with warm water, and mixed the little packet of powder that came with the roses. Then I uncapped the stems, cut them on the diagonal, and put them in the vase, intermingling the colors. I set them on the coffee table in the living room and stood back to admire them. When I had utterly filled myself with their delicate beauty, I went out to pick up my cake and a couple of Valentine cookies for Mel's kids.

So it was a special day. Jack thought the cognac was too good to drink, but I insisted he open it and give it a try. A man of taste, he pronounced it the best he had ever had. He told me he had wanted to get me a piece of jewelry, but he had no idea what I would like and I had never hinted at anything. (His mother hinted when she wanted something, and he thought all women did the same.) I had never thought about it, but I expect hinting isn't my style. As for jewelry, I have very little of my own, having spent almost half my life as a Franciscan nun, but what I have is very precious—my wedding ring, a small gold ring given to me by a lovely woman who lives on the west side of New York and whom I met when I investigated the murder of an old friend of hers, and a few pieces I inherited from my mother and my aunt. I am quite content with what I have, and I was happy Jack hadn't gone to great expense for something it had never occurred to me I needed.

The Gross children thought my heart-shaped cookies were the best they had ever tasted—although anything their mother bakes is probably superior—and the roses brightened our house for many days, reminding me of the love Jack and I feel for each other. All very nice, very romantic, the things that sweet memories are born of.

I was busy, as usual. On Tuesdays I taught my poetry course at a local college, and when I wasn't looking into one or another murder, I worked for my friend Arnold Gold, a lawyer with a practice in New York City. It was when I returned from the city after putting in a day at his office that I first learned about Carlotta French.

There was a message on my answering machine to call Amy Grant, an Oakwood woman I had met at meetings as well as socially. When I had my coat off, I called her.

There was a lot of small talk at the beginning of the conversation and I thought perhaps she just wanted to be neighborly, but after about five minutes, she said, "Do you remember meeting my old college roommate when you and Jack came over last fall?"

"Yes," I said, recalling a very pleasant evening. "Carlotta something."

"Carlotta French. She'd like to talk to you. Do you have a little time?"

I looked at my watch. It was six o'clock and Jack would be home for dinner, as it was Friday. "Not right now. I just walked in and I have some cooking to do."

"You think tomorrow?"

"What's this about?"

"I'd rather not say. It's a little complicated and I want her to do the talking. She remembers you very fondly from that evening."

I liked Amy and I remembered Carlotta well, kind of a vibrant person who did more in her life than I could ever contemplate doing in mine. "Maybe eleven tomorrow morning," I said, thinking that we'd be up and about by then, and if Jack were out doing his weekend thing in hardware stores and lumberyards, it would be a good time to hear Carlotta out.

"We'll be there at eleven," Amy said, and that was the end of our conversation.

* * *

I heard them coming up the walk just at eleven, and I set the paper aside and opened the door.

"Hi, Chris," Amy said, pulling off a beautiful fur hat. She stamped snow off her fashionable black boots and came in. "I'm sure you remember my friend, Carlotta French."

I said hello and took their coats. A gust of cold air had come in with them, and I shivered a little after the door closed. I hadn't made any coffee because I didn't want to encourage a long visit. I had things to do today, so the sooner we cleaned up the business of the meeting, the happier I would be.

"We appreciate your talking to us," Amy said. "Carlotta's a friend from college and she's staying with me for a while. It's really very good of you to give us your time."

"I have no idea what this is about," I said. They both had cold-reddened faces, as though they had walked in the street waiting for the appointed hour.

"It's me," Carlotta said. "I have a problem and no one will help me. I remember a story you told the night we met, and I thought you might be the one."

"You'll have to tell me about it."

"Yes." She looked over at the sofa where Amy was sitting. "You've heard this so many times you can tell it yourself, Amy. Why don't you leave Chris and me? I'll walk home when we're through. It's not that far."

I had the sense that Amy was somewhat disappointed, that she wanted to be part of whatever Carlotta was going to tell me, but she got up, patted her friend's shoulder, took her coat out of the closet where I had hung it less than five minutes ago, and left.

"It's about my husband," Carlotta said, when she had

sat down again. "I hate an audience. I hope I didn't hurt Amy's feelings—she's been so wonderful to me since this happened—but I think I'll do better one-on-one."

She was an attractive woman, a little shorter than I, with straight dark blond hair, cut fairly short. She was wearing a green suit with the jacket open over a cashmere sweater of a lighter shade of green. She was rather busty, which at first glance made her appear plump, but she was not. The straight skirt was slim and her legs were shapely.

"I'm listening."

"My husband is missing," she said. Then she shook her head. "It's a complicated story and every time I tell it, I seem to start somewhere else. It happened last week on St. Valentine's Day, and he's not the only person involved. There are two others."

"They're all missing?"

"Missing and presumed dead."

"I see."

"You really don't. Let me fill you in a little. My husband's name is Val, Valentine actually. He was born on Valentine's Day, and his family named him for the occasion. One way or another, almost everything of importance in his life has happened on that day. Among other things, it's our wedding anniversary."

"How long are you married?"

"Six years." She looked down at her hands. They were well manicured, the nails covered with natural polish. "He sent me red roses and this." She held out her right hand. On the ring finger was a beautiful ruby cut in the shape of a heart.

"It's wonderful. I've never seen anything like it."

"Nor I." She admired it for a moment, her face

clouded. "We had lunch on the fourteenth and he gave it to me. We were to have an anniversary dinner last Saturday, but he was gone by then."

"Where do you live, Carlotta?" I asked. "I don't remember if you told me."

"Upstate, not far from Buffalo. Val works near where we live and I work in the city, but my job involves a lot of travel. I had to be somewhere on the fifteenth, so after lunch, Val drove me to the airport and I flew to Chicago. If I'd stayed home, Val would still be with me."

The look on her face told me she blamed herself, in the way that people do when they believe that a chance act has stricken someone down. *If only I had called him back to answer the phone, he would not have been at the intersection when the bus went out of control.*

"Tell me about it."

"He has two friends who are as close as brothers. They grew up together, went to each other's weddings, cheered each other on through life. On Wednesday of last week they all celebrated Val's thirty-fifth birthday."

"How?"

"They were going to go out to dinner and then probably back to one of their houses. They did go to dinner. The police found that out the next day. I suspect at least one or two of them had a little too much to drink, although the restaurant didn't seem to think so. They had a record of the bill. But they didn't go back to anyone's house after dinner."

"Something happened?" I said.

"Until a few days before Valentine's Day it had been a very cold winter in western New York," Carlotta said. "The snow came early, and the temperature was so low for so long that it stayed around and was added to. Lake

Erie had been frozen for over a month, although it warmed up suddenly last week. It's been an ice skater's paradise. Apparently, the men decided to cross a narrow part of the lake on foot and end up in Canada."

"Oh, no."

"The car was found the next morning, and none of the three came home or showed up at work. Someone called the police and the county sent helicopters out to look for them, but there's no sign of life anywhere. We can't be sure all three made the trek because there was a light snow overnight, and any footprints they might have made were pretty much obliterated."

"How can you be sure they walked across the lake?"

"They talked about doing it at dinner and the waitress remembered it. Also, the car was found at the beach. There isn't much there besides the lake and no one in the area saw any of them. The helicopter found some breaks in the ice several miles from where they found the car, just where they would have been if they were hiking across to Canada." She stopped as though the thought were too painful. "There was a red cashmere scarf snagged on the ice. We gave a scarf like that to Matty last Christmas."

"Were they able to search the lake for bodies?"

"They tried, but the hole got bigger and the ice shifted, and they didn't find anything. Now they think it'll be spring before—before anything surfaces."

"Carlotta, tell me about your husband's friends."

"They're not like Val."

"But they're friends."

"You know how it is with people you grow up with, people who were in first grade with you, you just keep loving them even though your lives take different routes.

That's the way it's been with Val and Matty and Clark. Matty's never really succeeded at anything he's tried, but he has a father-in-law who keeps them going. Clark owns a hardware store in a suburb of Buffalo, a very big, successful store. He's a happy guy—or was."

"Married?"

"Both of them."

"But the dinner was just the men."

"That's the way it always was. They loved being together, making their own celebrations."

"What did Val do?"

"Val works with computers. He builds clones to fit clients' needs. He services them." She used the present tense with determination.

"What's happening now that he's not there?"

"His partner is running the business."

"When did you hear about the tragedy?"

"The next day, the fifteenth. My office called me. I flew back from Chicago, but there wasn't anything I could do."

"Whose car was found near the lake?"

"Matty's. He had a big four-wheel drive. Where he lives, you need one, and it's one of his big-boy's toys."

"Carlotta, I don't see where I fit in all this. I can't imagine what you want me to do."

"I have a theory." She crossed her legs. "I think the idea to walk across the lake was Matty's. Matty's crazy, always has been. He's a practical joker, a dare-taker. He makes me nervous, although I've always been careful what I said about him to Val. Clark is kind of a quiet guy, though when the three of them got together, they were always boisterous. I'm trying not to point a finger. I want to be fair. I've known these people—and their wives—

for as long as I've known Val. But if I had to make a judgment, I would say Matty said, 'Hey, let's walk across the lake to Canada. We may not have another chance for a lot of years.' And I think Clark probably went along with him because it's what Clark always did. But Val isn't stupid, he doesn't take chances, he's a grown-up, not just a big kid that dresses like a man. I don't think Val went with them."

"That's a big theory. Can you back it up?"

"Not with anything hard. But I know my husband. He knew the value of life, the value of our marriage. I don't think he'd take a chance like that."

"That's very interesting," I said. "But where is he if he didn't go with them?"

"That's what I want you to find out."

So that was the story, and I turned her down. She had no proof whatever that her husband had not drowned in the icy waters of Lake Erie on the night of Valentine's Day, nor had she any idea where he might go if he had not accompanied his friends. No one had heard a word from any of the three men since they had left the restaurant that night, and apparently, no one expected to. A university scientist predicted that the bodies would surface, if at all, in late May or possibly early June, depending on the water temperature, and until then, there was nothing anyone could do but wait. The other two wives, Carlotta told me, accepted their husbands' fate and presumed they were dead. One of them had had a funeral service for her husband a few days ago, but the other was waiting for the bodies to be recovered. It was a very sad affair, made worse by the not knowing, by the

12 Lee Harris

little ray of hope that lives in all of us when we cannot prove that the worst has happened.

I pressed Carlotta for reasons why her husband, if he were still alive, would not come home, but she had no answers for me. The story had come out smoothly until her bombshell; then it faltered. Would the other two men have crossed the lake without Val? She couldn't be sure. If Val had decided not to accompany them, why would he not have simply returned home? Well, the car wasn't his, but, of course, there were taxis, there were neighbors who might be persuaded to come out and pick him up, although none had come forward.

There was nothing to go on except her strong feeling that her husband was the smartest of the three and therefore still alive. I told her that wasn't enough for me and besides, I was involved in another investigation, I had my teaching, I had a husband I didn't want to leave. She was very understanding, and we agreed that if anything happened, if her husband or either of the others turned up somewhere, she would let me know. And when that time came in the spring, if indeed the bodies surfaced, I wanted to know about it.

She promised she would keep me informed, and she left a few minutes before twelve, before Jack returned from his Saturday morning ramblings among lumber and power tools.

Amy Grant called me twice, several weeks apart, to tell me that nothing had happened. And that was the last I heard until I answered the phone that beautiful spring day and heard Carlotta's voice.

2

There was a hopeful note in her voice as she said there had been an interesting surprise. "What happened?" I asked.

"Only two bodies have surfaced, Matty's and Clark's."

"Your husband's still missing?"

"Yes, and if his body doesn't turn up very soon, they're going to be out looking for him."

"Why? Couldn't it have gotten tangled in stuff at the bottom of the lake?"

"I suppose it could have, but there's something else I haven't told you. There's a bullet in Matty's body."

"He was shot?"

"Before he went into the water. So Val's a prime suspect."

"That is a shocker. Did Val own a gun?"

"Not that I ever knew about. The police have already run a check. He never registered one. Matty owned hunting guns, of course. He was a big hunter. It's why we gave him the red scarf for Christmas last year, so he wouldn't get himself shot. I guess it didn't work." It was a rather flip comment from a woman whose husband was a suspect in the murder.

"Do they know what kind of gun was used?" I asked.

13

"A handgun, not a hunting rifle. It's not likely he shot himself."

Not very, I thought. "You told me these three men loved each other like brothers. Could you have been wrong? Could there have been disagreements that might have led to murder?"

"How can I answer that?" she said. "How much does anyone know about any other person? But if there were, I didn't know about them because Val never said a word, and neither did the others that I ever heard about. And if they weren't getting along, why did they go out for dinner on Valentine's Day?"

"To set up an opportunity for murder," I said.

"If that's true, then Clark killed Matty, which is what I think happened. I told you in February I didn't think Val was part of the group on the ice and so far I've been proven right. I think the two men went together, got into a fight over something, and Clark shot Matty and they both went down together."

"What did they fight about?"

"I don't know."

"And why was Clark carrying a gun?"

"Chris, I want you to find the answers to all these questions. I think if you do, I'll find Val. And whatever happened on the lake that night, I want him back."

"I don't know, Carlotta. It's very intriguing. I have to admit I thought you were fantasizing that your husband didn't join the other two men that night, but it certainly looks as though you were right. I'd love to find out where he was that night, and why he didn't go with them, and what's become of him. It's just that my life has changed since February."

"Are you tied up in a job?"

"I'm pregnant."

"Oh, I see. That's wonderful," she said, almost as an afterthought.

"It is wonderful. I'm feeling fine and I expect to continue to, but I wonder if I just shouldn't stay close to home."

"This makes me feel very awkward," Carlotta said. "I don't want to press you. You have my number if you want to call, and you can leave a message on the machine if I'm not home. If you think you're feeling up to it, I'd really like you to take this on. The police have pretty much made up their minds that if Val doesn't turn up dead, he's a killer. It's not much of a choice for me. I think he's alive and I know he isn't a killer. If I could give up my job and look for him, I would, but I have to support myself. Will you think about it?"

"I will. Thanks for calling."

When I hung up, my mind was flooded with questions I wanted to ask. What had appeared to be a foolish venture by three old friends, possibly under the influence, had become much more, much more interesting and sinister. If, as it appeared most simply, Clark had killed Matty and in the scuffle both had broken through the ice, what had happened to Val? Had he witnessed the shooting and run? Had he been shot, too, and was his body stuck on something at the bottom of Lake Erie? Or had he managed to shoot Matty from a great enough distance that he could escape with his life, while poor Clark had stayed behind to help his friend and then died for his efforts? I wondered whether Clark had tried to pull Matty from the icy waters using the red scarf, only to be pulled in himself. But the question I could never get away from was what had happened to Val and where was he, dead or alive?

"Only two bodies?" Jack said, when we were sitting at the kitchen table for his late supper after returning from evening law classes.

"You sound as surprised as I am. When she told me all that stuff in February, I thought she was dreaming."

"Where did Carlotta say she was when all this disaster happened?"

"Chicago, I think. Anyway, on a business trip. Val took her to the airport after they had lunch together."

"I suppose it's true," Jack said. "Her company would have called her there to tell her the news—if they knew before she got back that her husband was missing and presumed drowned. But you know the drill, Chris. Check the items you can verify, establish facts, then go on to the rest of it."

"You think she's involved in those deaths?"

"You know me. I don't think anything, not at this point anyway. It's too early to be thinking. It's evidence-collecting time. But that's one weird story." He filled his plate again. "So a dumb prank by a trio of men who should have known better turns out to be a homicide. I don't have to ask you if you're interested."

"Carlotta wants me to look into it. She says the police have decided that if Val isn't dead in the lake, he's a living murderer."

"Pretty obvious assumption. But she's holding out for a third possibility, right?"

"Right."

"Alive and innocent. So why did he run? And did he

run before or after the killing? Does he know there's been a killing?"

"If he didn't know when he ran, he must have found out about it soon after. It was in the papers, on TV. He couldn't really have missed it."

"Unless he went far away, maybe out of the country. But what did he use for money?"

"I haven't asked Carlotta about bank accounts, but I'd guess the police are looking into that now. And I wonder if she can tell if he stopped off at home to pick up some clothes before he left. Maybe he went home, Jack. Maybe he's home, he goes to sleep, he wakes up the next morning, ready to go to work, and turns on the news."

"They don't know about it yet, Chris. It's too early. True, the men didn't return home, but I'll bet that wasn't the first time. Their wives may even have been used to it, may have been waiting for their husbands to toddle home after a hard night at the bar rail. It takes awhile to make the decision that he should have been home a couple of hours ago. So wife number one calls wife number two and finds out both the husbands are missing. Wife number three, of course, is on a business trip so no one reaches her. But no one answers at her house, so the other two wives know husband number three isn't home either."

"But when the three men don't show up for work, everyone gets the message and someone calls the police." I got up and brought the coffee to the table. "And that's when everyone starts to panic." I poured and brought over a box of store-bought cookies. "So that means that if Val went home, he didn't answer the phone when the other wives called, which is suspicious in itself, or he was already gone by morning."

"I love it," Jack said. "And you do, too."

"I do. I wonder if anyone took Carlotta seriously in February when she said she didn't think her husband would have crossed the lake with the others. That would have been the time to check the taxi companies and the buses. It's months later now, and no bus driver would remember a particular passenger that rode his bus on February fourteenth. A taxi driver might, though, especially if he saw pictures on the news of the men who were missing. If Val was trying to disappear, I think he would have gotten on a bus to anywhere rather than take a taxi to his home."

"That makes sense," Jack said. "It also means he planned this disappearance, making him look like a good suspect for the homicide. You want to take this on?"

"I don't know."

"Sure you know. You're just worrying about what I'm worrying about."

A bit of tissue that was half his and half mine and would be our first child before year's end. "Maybe I should ask the doctor."

"What's she going to tell you? That flying in a plane and doing some legwork won't hurt, and the exercise is good for you?"

I smiled. "Probably."

"How do you feel?"

"As good as the day I met you."

"You nervous?"

"Yes, I'm nervous. I'm not nervous about going to teach my class or driving to the supermarket. It's just that this is so new and so important, and I keep thinking that I'm over thirty and maybe that makes a difference."

"Did you talk to Dr. Campbell about it?"

"She said she was exactly my age when she had her first child."

"So there you are."

"You sound like you're encouraging me."

"Chris, we both know you're going to do this."

"We do?"

"Don't we?"

I shook my head. "Maybe we've been married too long."

He leaned across the table and kissed me. "Not long enough. Just watch out for our mutual interest."

3

Carlotta, of course, was very happy that I had decided
to give the case a try. She saw my job as finding Val,
dead or alive, wherever he was. I saw it from a larger per-
spective, figuring out who had killed Matty and, if possible, why, and also, because there had to be some
connection, what Val's role in all of this was. I was pretty
sure that answers to any of the questions would lead to
answers to all. The first thing I wanted to do, I told Carlotta, besides reading everything in the papers about the
Valentine's Day walk across the lake and the recent discovery of the bodies, was to talk to all three wives.

"I'll get us all together as soon as you arrive," she said.

I said, "Great," and regretted it almost immediately.
"On second thought, it might be better if I speak to all of
you separately."

"Why is that?" she said with a wary edge in her voice.

"Because although you may have been best friends
before February fourteenth, there's a large possibility
now that one of the husbands killed another of them—or
even two of them—and that may not sit well with the
survivors."

"Whatever you say." But I thought she sounded disappointed, as though she had hoped to hear what the other

wives had to say, or perhaps because she had thought she was directing the investigation and now realized that could not be. "When do you think you can come?"

"I teach a class on Tuesday, and we're coming to the end of the semester pretty soon. I don't want to fly up tomorrow and rush back on Monday. Let's say I'll come up next Wednesday and stay till the following Monday, if I have to. In the meantime, if anything happens," I was sure she knew what I meant, "let me know. I can always cancel the flight."

"You still think Val's body will surface, don't you?"

"I don't know what to think. I have so many questions I'll probably go nonstop for days. One of the people I want to talk to is your husband's business partner."

"Why?"

Again there was the edge to her voice. "Carlotta, partners are intimates. Whether they love or hate each other, they know a lot about each other. If a man is making—or getting—phone calls, his partner is sure to be aware of it. Sometimes mail is sent to the business address instead of the home address. I have to know these things. If you have a problem with any of this—"

"No, of course not. I just hadn't really thought about what an investigation entails. When the men disappeared in February, it was assumed to be an accident and the police hardly questioned me. I just have to get used to looking at this differently. I'll cooperate with anything you want to do, Chris. There won't be any problems. And you'll stay with me, if that's all right."

"It's fine."

"I have a big house, and you can use Val's car. I start it every once in awhile to keep the battery going. It's in good shape and it'll be better when it's driven."

"Then I'll see you next Wednesday?"

"Yes. I'll get you a plane before noon, and I'll pick you up myself at the Buffalo airport."

"And you'll arrange for me to talk to Val's partner."

"I'll call him right away."

I must admit to an immediate surge in my spirits. Not only was it spring, with all the pleasure that the fresh air and sunshine give me, but I was embarking on one of those great journeys I had come to look forward to in the last two years, digging for information, development of a theory, and finding who knew what—a killer or killers, a victim or victims, a reason, a motive, an explanation I could not begin to imagine on the day I began.

And more than that, I sensed it was my last case, at least for a long time. With a baby coming I would not be hopping on a plane to go anywhere, not even picking up and going into the city for a day. I knew about as little about babies as one could at my age; I had never had anything to do with them after an occasional job as a sitter when I was young, and I had sat only with children whom I could talk to. Diapers were a mystery. I was aware that they had been transformed from cotton to disposable only because I saw shelves of them in the local supermarket and occasionally caught an ad on TV. I had a lot to learn, and I would do it at home with my child.

I told my friend and neighbor Melanie Gross that I would be leaving for a few days and sketched out the little I knew. Like me, she was excited and intrigued, not to mention very encouraging about taking on an adventure while pregnant.

"I worked till the last minute with my first," she said. "And that meant getting up, driving to school, and teaching a full schedule, a lot of it on my feet. Don't worry, and drink lots of milk."

It sounded like good advice, the second half of it perhaps easier to follow. I called Amy Grant and told her I was flying to Buffalo and would stay with Carlotta for a few days. She had already heard the news about the surfacing of the bodies and she wished me luck. In this case I interpreted luck to mean that Carlotta's husband would not be involved in the homicide—and would turn up alive. Maybe, I thought, packing my bag on Tuesday night, it was too much to hope for.

Spring travels north a few miles a day, and even from the air I could see it had barely reached western New York. In Oakwood the trees had all leafed out; here the buds were just breaking and the air was cool but steeped with the promise of spring. I walked up the long corridor to where a small crowd waited for New York City passengers, and there was Carlotta, her eyes searching the faces of the moving group until she recognized mine.

"Chris, you made it," she said, coming forward, and I wondered if she had doubted that I would come.

We shook hands. "Everything is scaled down compared to the big city. It must be nice to live in a less populated area."

"It is. And everything's close. Did you check a bag?"

"Yes." I was carrying a small one and when she saw it, she took it from me.

"Right downstairs. Then we'll go out to the car. It's a bit of a drive, but we'll stop for lunch on the way. I've got you scheduled for later this afternoon, if that's all right."

"It's fine. I'm here and I want to get started."

The suitcase came around on the belt and Carlotta grabbed it, leaving me with two free hands and not a little embarrassment. But when I protested, she would hear none of it.

"I brought Val's car," she said, as we walked into the parking lot, small by New York City standards but nowhere near as full. "It drives like a dream. I think you'll enjoy it."

"What kind of car is it?"

"A Mercedes. There it is."

"Carlotta, I can't drive a car like that."

"Why? Because it's expensive? It drives like any other car. Put your foot on the accelerator and push. That's all there is to it."

"It's funny. I asked Jack once if he wanted an expensive car, and he said maybe someday."

"Val wanted it now. He wanted everything now. He earned it and he got it. I hope he'll come home to enjoy it all again."

She stowed my luggage in the trunk and we were off. We stopped somewhere for a light lunch, and she smiled when I ordered milk with my sandwich.

"We decided to wait to have children," she said.

"I was just married last year, so this is my first opportunity. I think I told you last fall, I was a nun till two years ago. I never thought I'd have children, so it's a real bonus for me."

"Then this may be your last case for a long time."

"Maybe," I hedged. "I haven't even gotten to the point where I need maternity clothes. I can't think that far ahead."

"Just find Val," she said. "Then you can retire."

* * *

On the way to her house she took a detour and stopped at the point where Matty's four-wheel drive had been found the day after the men disappeared. I haven't traveled much, and the Great Lakes were completely new to me. If you had told me I was standing at the edge of the Atlantic Ocean, I would have believed it. The lake was vast, and the wind blowing off it, cold. Like the strip of beach on the Long Island Sound near my own home, this one had the cold, deserted look of off-season. The water was darkly forbidding, waves and whitecaps everywhere and the water slapping the shore as though angry.

"It's a great place to swim in the summer," Carlotta said. "I know it's hard to imagine it covered with ice and snow, but it gets that way when we have a cold winter. What happened this year around Valentine's Day is that we had a few warm days, and I guess the ice started to melt, not around here or they wouldn't have gotten as far as they did."

"It's possible a gunshot may have gotten a hole started."

"That's possible, too."

"Where was their vehicle?"

"Right where I've parked."

"Was it locked?"

"I'm pretty sure it was. Matty's wife, Annie, had to find the extra key."

"Anything left inside?"

She composed herself before she answered. "Val's watch was in the backseat. It was a very fine watch. He was probably afraid of falling and damaging it."

She had not told me that before, not indicated in any way that Val had been with the other two men on the beach. "So we know he came this far," I said.

"This far, yes."

I didn't say it out loud, but it certainly looked to me as though Val must have made the trek with the others. If he were going to leave them at this point, why would he leave his expensive watch behind?

"I know what you're thinking," Carlotta said. "You think he went with them. I think he took his watch off and walked across the beach with the others. Maybe he even started walking on the ice with them and then turned back when his head cleared, but it was too late to retrieve his watch because the car was locked. He assumed he'd pick it up in the morning."

"Did he go home?" I asked. "Were you able to find any indication that he went to the house, packed a bag, took a toothbrush, and then left?"

"I don't know."

"You mean it's possible."

"It's possible. I know he didn't take a toothbrush; I would have noticed that. But I never counted how many pairs of socks he had, how many sets of underwear, how many casual shirts. Is a navy blue shirt missing? I don't know. I know which jacket he was wearing that night because it's not in the closet, and I'm pretty sure he was wearing his snow boots because they're gone, too. Aside from that, I'm just not sure."

"What did he wear when he took you out to lunch?"

"A suit. It's in his closet."

"So he went home and changed after he took you to the airport."

"Sure. All three of them probably went casual."

We turned away from the lake and walked back to the car.

"You said it snowed that night," I said.

"A little. Enough to obliterate any footprints. And there was a wind, so the snow may have drifted a little. When a police car stopped next to Matty's car, the cop pretty much trampled the area."

I smiled in spite of myself. "My husband says the police do more to destroy crime scenes than anyone else does. The cop didn't know anyone was missing at that point, so he had no reason to be careful where he walked. Anyway, if Val came back from the lake, he may have walked across another part of the beach. He had no reason to return to the car if it was locked."

"It's so frustrating," Carlotta said. "I've gone over and over all of this since Valentine's Day." She looked down at the heart-shaped ruby ring on her right hand. "A man doesn't give his wife a gift like this at lunch and disappear after dinner without a word."

I had to admit it seemed unlikely. She unlocked the car and we got in.

"How did he pay for it?" I asked, as she backed up.

"It must have been cash. I never got a bill for it."

"That's a lot of cash to carry around."

"It's what we've always done. We both work, and when we buy each other gifts, we use our own money. We both have bank accounts in our own names."

"Has his been used since February fourteenth?"

"The bankbooks are in his desk drawer. They haven't been touched. And he hasn't written any checks."

That would be easy enough to check. "Any credit cards?"

"I have those records, too. Although some of the papers for the company credit card may be at the office."

"Did you keep much cash in the house?"

"Never. We both thought it wasn't safe. There's no

home safe either. We keep valuables in a box in the bank."

"What about insurance, Carlotta?"

She looked blank. "Nothing that I know about."

"Maybe something will turn up."

When Carlotta finally pulled into the driveway, I couldn't help being impressed with her house. It was large and had a lot of land, a rather extravagant residence for two people who spent a lot of time away from it. We went in through the garage and stopped in the large foyer to hang our coats in the closet. The foyer rose two stories with high windows that let in natural light.

"It's beautiful," I said.

"Thank you. We put a lot of ourselves into this house. There's still more we want to do, but it's on its way. Come upstairs and I'll show you your room."

"My" room was furnished comfortably for a guest with a double bed, a dresser, a lamp I would read by, a big closet, and my very own bathroom. I promised Carlotta I would be down as soon as I had hung up a few clothes. Before I opened my suitcase, though, I went to the large window, opened the blinds, and looked out. The land behind the house was as well cared-for as the front and appeared to amount to a couple of acres. There were flower beds, tall trees, younger trees that had probably been planted since the young couple moved in, and a stone patio that would surely be graced with summer furniture when the weather became warmer.

I found my way to the kitchen where Carlotta was sitting at a built-in table looking over her mail. "When do we begin?" I said.

She looked at her watch. "Pretty soon. Clark's wife,

Bambi, is first on the list. I have to call to see whether she wants to come here or wants you there." She reached for the telephone and stopped. "A message. Let me listen first. Whenever there's a message, I think it might be Val."

She pressed a button and the tape rewound, a sound that always reminded me of scurrying mice. Then a voice said, "Carlotta, this is Bambi. I've changed my mind. I really don't want to talk to your friend. I've spent hours with the police and I'm worn out. I don't know what she can do anyway. So let's cancel."

"I can't believe it," Carlotta said. "She must be getting worried that the police think Clark killed Matty. This is very disappointing."

"Let's not worry about it. There are plenty of other things I can do."

"Let me call Annie Franklin. She'll talk to you. She's looking forward to it."

I walked into the windowed breakfast room as she made her call. This was a bright, sunny house, one I would enjoy living in. Jack and I had decided to build a huge addition onto our house which would give us a family room for the first time, and a wonderful bedroom above it. Without meaning to, I had become interested in other people's houses, how they arranged furniture, how they added on rooms. When I had moved into Aunt Meg's house, I thought it would remain the way it was forever, but I had never imagined my life would change as much as it had. When my baby was born, we would have a bigger, more comfortable house, another fireplace, an extra bathroom. I had come a long way from my small cell at St. Stephen's, my brown Franciscan habit, my shorn hair, and my simple life shared with a group of women.

"She'd rather have you go over there," Carlotta said, bringing me back to the case at hand. "She can't get a sitter."

"That's fine. You can point me in the right direction."

"You were right about relationships going sour. Annie's not very anxious to spend time with Bambi. Bambi's been giving her a hard time since the bodies surfaced."

"I can understand that."

"Those men didn't hate each other, Chris. They were friends. I know you have to be suspicious of everyone and everything that happened, but I think I'm a pretty good judge of character. They loved each other."

"Did the wives?"

She didn't answer right away. "No, the wives didn't. We didn't dislike each other, but we weren't best friends. We got along. We spent a lot of time with each other because of our husbands, but I think each of us has a best friend outside the group. I know I do."

"What time am I expected there?"

"I rescheduled for four since Bambi backed out. That gives you more than an hour. It's a ten-minute drive."

"I'd like to look at Val's desk."

"Come with me."

4

It turned out that Val had a home office complete with the expected computer, floor-to-ceiling bookshelves filled mostly with books on his professional interest, a small radio, a telephone with buttons that automatically dialed a host of locations both personal and business-related, and more packages of software than I had ever seen outside a store.

I know very little about computers and if Val had life secrets stored on his, I would have to get an expert in to help me. But for a first look I had other things in mind, and I sat down at the desk and began to open drawers. The bankbooks were in the first drawer I opened, and I took them out. There were three, each book a different color, each account at a different bank. I slid the first one out of the plastic envelope and opened it. It had pages of entries, both deposits and withdrawals, but many more of the former than the latter. I flipped to the last page and saw that the final balance was over ninety-seven thousand dollars. I took a breath. Rather a lot of cash, I thought, considering that interest rates were low. The last transaction was a withdrawal on February twelfth, two days before Val's disappearance. He had taken over three thousand dollars out of the bank, probably, I thought, for

Carlotta's ruby ring, a pricey gift but one he could obviously afford.

I went backwards through the pages and noticed that whenever the balance approached one hundred thousand, he would remove funds to bring the amount below that figure. From somewhere I recalled that bank accounts were insured up to that crucial number, so perhaps he took the funds and invested them elsewhere to keep the whole amount insured. It would seem to be a good idea.

I slipped the book back in its case and took out the second one. This account was handled very differently from the first. Here there were periodic withdrawals in even amounts, one hundred, two hundred, seven hundred. I flipped to the last page and saw that the last withdrawal had been made on February second. Prior to that, the last deposit, a thousand dollars, had been made at the end of January. I opened the first book again and checked the last few entries. Sure enough, a thousand dollars had been withdrawn from book number one on the same day a deposit had been made in book number two, and for the same amount. It seemed that Val put his overflow from the first account into the second account, or something like that.

I took the last book out of its case and opened it to the last page. Like the other two it had a large balance, over ninety thousand dollars. All told, the three books had nearly three hundred thousand dollars all together, a princely sum from my point of view. Like the second book, this one had frequent withdrawals in even amounts and more occasional deposits. I worked backwards, noting that the balance was always held over ninety thousand. When I came to the first page, I saw the name of the passbook owner for the first time, Valentine Krassky. Val and Carlotta had different last names.

A red light on the phone caught my eye. In another part of the house, Carlotta was using the line. I turned back to my task. There seemed to be no address book in the desk, but a large Rolodex sat on the top at arm's length from where I sat. I flipped through it for a few minutes, finding Carlotta's number at work, Clark's and Matty's work and home numbers, Matty's work number crossed out and changed several times since the card had first been written. If this reflected his work history, he had held a number of jobs.

Most of the names and addresses appeared to be work-related—I didn't see anything that looked like a plumber or electrician, so that was probably Carlotta's domain—and I left the Rolodex and turned to the papers on his desk. There were letters that Val had stamped with "Received Date," and which I assumed he had yet to answer. He seemed to be a neat, well-organized man. All the unanswered letters had arrived within a week of his disappearance. Probably all the earlier ones had already been answered and filed away. From what I could see, these were not personal correspondence, but those having to do with business and with the kinds of things computer people have fun with. None of it made much sense to me.

I was replacing the unanswered letters in their neat pile when Carlotta came in. She had changed into jeans and a pale blue cashmere turtleneck that gave her a look of casual sophistication. A long string of blue beads interspersed with silver added a note of eye-catching luxury.

"How're you doing?"

"I discovered you and Val have different last names."

"I forgot to mention that. You and your husband do, too, don't you?"

"A little inconsistently," I admitted. "I answer to almost anything."

"So do I. I'd been at my job several years when we married, and I have no brothers to carry on the family name. I decided to be the one."

"I've been looking at names and addresses and bank balances," I said. "Val kept a lot of cash in his accounts."

"I think he needed to, psychologically I mean. He came from a family that had very little, and it made him feel secure to know that there was plenty of cash around. Even this—" she held up the beautiful ruby heart on her right hand— "made him feel good. He wanted to be able to do rash things with money if he chose to. It gave him a high."

"But you don't think walking across Lake Erie gave him that kind of a high."

"It didn't. Val was rational. He wouldn't put his life in jeopardy to be able to say, 'I skated over to Canada.' "

"Well, there's plenty of money in these three bank accounts if he wanted it."

"He hasn't tried to take it out. I called the detective on the case when I went upstairs. He's checked all three banks. I gave him the account numbers last week."

"So Val kept all this cash in case he needed it, and he hasn't taken any out." I didn't have to say the obvious. "Something else. I found several unanswered letters that seem to have technical information in them. I would think someone as comfortable with computers as Val would do most of his correspondence on the computer. E-mail, I think it's called."

"He did, but e-mail isn't secure. Those letters contain

information that's private, or even secret. He wouldn't want to pass it along except in a sealed envelope."

"So he uses the computer for chatting with friends and maybe making lunch dates, but puts his important ideas in the regular mail."

"That's just what he does." Carlotta looked at her watch. "Let me tell you how to get to Annie's house."

Annie's house was also large, but it was in a more built-up neighborhood and had less land. I parked on the street and walked up the concrete path to the front door. She must have been waiting just inside because as I rang, the door opened.

Annie Franklin was tall and slim. She looked like a woman who took good care of herself. Her fingernails were long, well-shaped, and glossed with a dark color I did not find attractive, but which was probably the season's best seller. She was wearing a white silk blouse with a big collar and brown pants with pleats. Her hair was long and just a little redder than brown. A couple of bracelets on one wrist jingled slightly when she moved.

We exchanged names and I gave her my condolences.

"Thank you." She took my coat and hung it in a nearby closet. "Let's sit in the garden room." She started for the back of the house and I followed her. The garden room was half glass with potted plants of many different kinds soaking up the plentiful sun. I told her how beautiful it was as we sat.

"It's even nicer with the doors open, but it's too cool today for that. Can I get you some pop? I'm not a coffee drinker so I don't keep it around."

"I'm fine, thanks. I'd just like to talk to you a little about what happened."

"Why is Carlotta doing this?" she said.

"She wants to find her husband. I think that's the whole answer."

"Where does she think he is?"

"I don't think she has any idea. She thinks he went away somewhere that night, February fourteenth, and hasn't come back for whatever reason."

"It's a little naive, don't you think?"

"I think she loves him and wants to believe he's still alive."

"Where would he be?" Annie said, her shoulders rising slightly as though she could not imagine.

"Maybe recovering from the shock of hearing what happened to his two best friends."

"He didn't strike me as a guy who would go off the deep end."

"How did he strike you?"

"Tough, smart, not much of a risk-taker."

"Then you don't believe he crossed the lake with the others?"

"I think he did. I think he pulled the trigger and ended up going down with the others."

"Why would he kill your husband, Annie?"

Her eyes filled. "Maybe Matty just got to be too much for him."

"In what way?" I felt excitement rising inside me. Carlotta had been so low-key, so even-handed in everything she said. This woman was loaded with opinions and not at all reticent about expressing them.

"Val had his eye on me," she said. "For years."

My excitement turned to instant distaste. The last thing I wanted was to get involved in a game of musical chairs among the three couples. "Did Carlotta know?" I asked.

"Carlotta wouldn't have believed it if you'd drawn her a map."

"Was there an affair between the two of you?" I asked, wanting to get as much as possible out in the open.

She shook her head slowly. "Never. I was married to the world's greatest man. Matty was the handsomest, most exciting guy I ever knew. Val was nothing compared to him."

"Do you and Carlotta get along well?"

"What did she tell you? That we were the best of friends? We weren't. We couldn't stand each other. We tolerated each other for the sake of our husbands."

"Does that include Bambi?"

"It includes Bambi most of all. I hear she won't even talk to you."

"That's right."

"She knows either her husband or Carlotta's pulled the trigger, and it looks more like hers since they've found the two bodies together. It's got her down."

"But you don't sound as though you blame her or her husband. You blame Carlotta's."

"Clark could have done it," she said, crossing her long legs. "I just can't think why he would."

"Did your husband own a handgun?"

"Matty was a hunter. He hunted animals, not people. He owned several rifles and he enjoyed using them. I don't think he ever had a handgun in his possession."

"Annie, did the men know that the women didn't like each other much?"

"Matty knew. I told him."

"How often did all of you get together?"

"Maybe once a month. Maybe less. The guys talked to

each other all the time. They didn't need us to stay close."

"You've given me two nice thumbnail descriptions of Matty and Val. Can you do it for Clark?"

She smiled as though I had complimented her. "Clark's easy. Simple, uncomplicated, never dreamed of anything he couldn't achieve with a little hard work. He had a business that he owned, a wife who loved him, a couple of kids, and a nice house. Clark was a happy man."

"Was Matty happy?"

Her face darkened a little. "We were happy with each other," she said. "But there was a lot he wanted that he didn't have."

"Like what?"

"His own business. He was going to start one with a couple of friends just before he died."

"This must be very hard for you, Annie."

She nodded and her eyes filled again. "We should have had another forty years together." She got up and walked back into the house proper, returning a moment later with something in her hand. "Have you ever seen pictures of the three men?"

"No."

"Here's one we took last summer. You've got my thumbnail sketches. Pick them out for me."

I took the frame and looked at the five-by-seven horizontal picture of three men in bathing suits on a beach. She was right. I could pick them out from her descriptions. "That's Matty in the middle."

"Right. You ever see a more gorgeous hunk of man?"

I smiled. The man on the left had to be Val, only because I was sure the one on the right was Clark. The latter was slim and good-looking, shorter than Matty and thinner than Val. Val was huskier, starting to lose his hair. All three were laughing, all were wet, all had their arms around their buddies' shoulders.

"Clark's the one on the right," I said.

"You got it. And Val's the guy on the left with his head somewhere else. He's probably putting a computer together while he's standing there." She took the picture from me and stared at it. "That's the same beach they left from on Valentine's Day. They found Matty's car there the next day."

"When did you know something was wrong?"

"When I woke up on the fifteenth. I called Bambi and she was getting nervous."

"Did either of you call Carlotta?"

"I think maybe I did."

"What happened?"

"She was out of town."

"Did Val answer?"

She looked at me as though I had misunderstood the situation. "Val was dead. How could he have answered?"

"We don't really know that he's dead. There's a possibility he didn't cross the lake, that he came home, went to sleep, and then left when he heard the news."

"He didn't answer," she said. "Nobody answered."

"Did you leave a message?"

"I don't remember. I may have hung up before the machine came on."

That would mean she had only let it ring three or four times.

"If I called at all," she said, while I was thinking it over. "That wasn't the best morning of my life. A lot of it's just a blur."

"Who called the police?" I asked.

"Maybe both of us. You'll have to ask Bambi. I know I did."

"When?"

She thought about it. "I had to get the kids off to school and I didn't want them to worry. Maybe I called after they left."

"Did you have any idea what had happened?"

She shook her head. "They were going out to celebrate Val's birthday. You know he was born on Valentine's Day."

"Yes."

"It was their anniversary, too. Did she tell you that?"

"Yes."

"But she had to go out of town so just the guys got together. Matty told me they were having dinner at Giordano's. It's an Italian restaurant everyone goes to. He walked out the door and I never saw him again." She looked beaten down as she said it.

"He never hinted they might walk across the lake?"

"Do I look like I'd stand for that?"

"Why do you think they did it, Annie?"

"I suppose Matty dared them. It's the kind of thing he'd do. It was a challenge. Matty's life was full of challenges. He took them on, one after the other."

"Do you think one of the other men brought a gun along to kill Matty?"

"I don't know what to think," she said. "I know I told you I believed Val did it, but how can I know for sure? What I'm sure of is that whoever had the gun must have had it with him when they went to dinner. From Giordano's, it's not far to the beach. It would have been out of the way to drive one of the guys home to pick something up."

"He might not have been wearing the right shoes," I suggested. "Or a warm enough jacket."

"Then it had to be Val. Matty never came back here, and Bambi would know if Clark came back."

"So it looks like it was premeditated."

"Doesn't it," she said.

"We just don't know why."

I pushed the button on the remote control and the garage door lifted smoothly. The car fitted its allotted space perfectly, and another push on the button closed the door behind me.

Carlotta was in the living room reading a book. She closed it and looked up as I came in.

"She talked pretty freely," I said. "She wasn't what I expected."

"People rarely are. Do you want to rest for a while?"

It took a moment before I remembered I was pregnant. "I'm fine," I said. "I'd just like to leave a message for my husband on our answering machine. Let him know I arrived."

"Sure. Whenever you're ready, we can go out to dinner. I made a reservation, but we don't have to stick to it. You like Italian food?"

"Love it."

"You're in for a treat. We're going to Giordano's."

5

It was the kind of place where you could wear whatever made you comfortable, where you recognized friends as you walked in, where the waitress knew you and was glad to see you. We were shown to a table for four, and two of the place settings were whisked away as we sat.

"This is the table they sat at," Carlotta said, and I felt a chill. "Their waitress is here tonight. You'll be able to talk to her. I'll leave the two of you alone if you'd like."

"Let's see how it goes," I said.

"Drink?"

"I guess not."

"Oh, of course."

"I've never been much of a drinker, but my doctor warned me off alcohol. And since it makes me sleepy more than anything else, it's not much of a loss."

"You don't mind if I indulge?"

"Not at all."

She ordered Scotch on the rocks with a twist and turned to me. "Do I get to hear about your conversation with Annie?"

"Sure. No conflict of interest that I can see. She seems savvy and open and full of opinions."

42

"Which she tosses out without much coaxing."

"That's about it. She wavered a little on whether Clark or Val killed Matty, but she comes down heavier on Val."

"Why not? He's missing."

"She says Val had his eye on her. For years."

"Oh, Annie." Carlotta sighed. "She can't live without it, the feeling that she's the center of attention whenever men are around, that everyone else's husband would rather have her than his own wife. It really gets boring, but she never lets up."

"Then you're pretty sure there's nothing there."

"Absolutely certain."

"You don't like her very much, do you?"

"Oh, she has her good points." Carlotta sipped her drink. "I guess we all do."

"Maybe Annie was the one who had an eye on your husband," I suggested. "Not the other way around."

"That's possible. Val introduced her to Matty."

"Val dated her first?"

"Val knew her. I don't think they dated."

"Were they all high school friends?"

"Annie came from somewhere else. When she was older."

"What about you?" I asked. "How did you meet Val?"

"We met skiing." She smiled. "Just like in books. It was a great love story. I couldn't have improved upon it." She looked up. A waitress was standing at her side. "Shall we order? If I get started talking, I'll go on all night."

The menu was so long that I turned to the board with the daily specials and picked a veal dish. It was offered in medium and large sizes, and I resisted the waitress's attempts to get me to order the large. When the dish came, I knew I had made the right decision.

"Do I get to hear the love story?" I asked.

"With pleasure. A friend and I decided to spend the weekend at a ski resort. I met Val my first time on the slopes. I liked the way he looked, and I guess he felt the same about me. We had a cup of coffee, and we both knew there was magic there. We spent the whole weekend talking. When we left on Sunday, I couldn't imagine spending the rest of my life without him."

"That was very quick, a weekend."

"Everything in our lives was quick. We met by accident, we fell in love over a cup of coffee, and he was taken away from me in the blink of an eye."

"You didn't meet on Valentine's Day, did you?"

"No, it was a weekend in January. And we didn't get married till the following year. But I think we knew that first Valentine's Day that we were meant for each other. We were brimming over with love. And it never flagged, Chris. We wove our lives together. We had different talents, different professional interests, but our relationship was the core of our existence."

She was very persuasive. I found myself imagining the two of them in ski clothes, red-cheeked and grinning, snow all over. I could see the progression as it took place from first looks to first words to what necessarily followed each. I not only believed Carlotta; I wanted to believe her. I didn't want to think that Annie Franklin had come between this couple, that on the night of his birthday and anniversary Val had had it out on the frozen lake with his friend, Annie's husband, that he had shot Matty so that he could have Annie. Could the same man that loved Carlotta have been wooed away by Annie? I found it hard to believe.

The meal was sumptuous. The main dish was accompanied by spaghetti and a plate of fried zucchini that we shared. A covered basket had a small loaf of garlic bread. If I were eating this meal in Oakwood, I would take home enough to keep me going for a day or two.

As I was twisting some spaghetti on my fork, a man walked over to the table and said, "Evening, Mrs. Krassky."

Carlotta looked up. "Chief, hi. Chris, this is Chief of Police Hellman. Chief, this is my friend Chris Bennett Brooks. We're putting our heads together to find Val."

"Well, I wish you both luck. You find anything out, you know where to find me."

"You'll be the first to know," Carlotta said.

Chief Hellman gave me a smile and a nod, patted Carlotta's shoulder, and walked away.

"I guess you don't eat out incognito any more."

"Not since Valentine's Day. The chief's in here all the time. I knew him by sight for years, but I never met him till the accident."

"It must be tough, knowing he suspects your husband of murder."

"It's tough on Bambi, too. I've thought about it a lot, as you can imagine. If we never find Val, we'll never know the truth. And suppose we do find him, will anyone believe him if he says he's innocent?"

"Let's not think about that now. Let's just try to find him."

"I think Peggy's coming over to talk to you. The

waitress," she explained. "I think I'll just go over to the bar and sit there while you talk."

Before I had time to say anything, she left, and the waitress who had been serving us came over and sat down at one of the unset places.

"I'm Peggy," she said. "Carlotta said you wanted to talk to me."

"I'm Chris. Thank you for helping. I'm trying to find Val. I want to know everything you can remember about those three men that night."

"I'll tell you what I remember," she said. "They were in here a lot." She was a thin woman in her forties, her skin pale, her lipstick very red, her hair an unnatural shade of blond. "Everybody knew them. I could tell you what they liked to drink, what they would and wouldn't eat. I still can't believe it happened."

"How long did you know them?"

"Years. I've been working here half my life. My cousin owns the place. They started coming here when they were kids in their twenties. Val had more hair then, Clark was a little thinner. Matty didn't change much. He was the cutest guy you ever laid eyes on." She smiled as though the image pleased her.

"Did you know them outside the restaurant?"

"Me? No. I have a cousin who once dated Clark. She should've married him. Maybe this wouldn't've happened."

"Tell me about that night."

"It was like any other night. They walked in, waved to me, and came over to this table. They always sat in my section if there was a table free. I brought them drinks and took their order."

"How much did they drink?"

"One apiece. Clark always had a bottle of beer. Val drank Johnnie Black. Matty had something fancy, a Rusty Nail, I think. One had chicken, one had veal, one had the osso bucco special."

"What kind of mood were they in?"

"They were always in a good mood, those guys. It was Val's birthday that day, did you know?"

"Carlotta told me."

"One of the others kinda whispered it to me when they came in, and I brought little cakes to the table with a candle for Val and we all sang. Can you believe he died on his birthday?"

"Did you hear any of the conversation, Peggy?"

"Some. It was friendly stuff. They were talking about a summer vacation, I think, where they would go. Matty talked about his new car, that big four-wheel drive they found at the beach the next day. And they talked about going down to the lake and playing ice hockey."

"Is that what they said? That they would play ice hockey on the lake?"

"I think that's what it was. They wanted to clown around. That's the way it sounded to me."

"Did anyone say anything about walking across the lake to Canada?"

She stopped and looked uncomfortable. "Yeah, I think so. Remember, I only heard bits and pieces of what they were saying. I was in and out of the kitchen, I had a bunch of other tables I was serving. I didn't hear a lot of whole sentences, you know what I mean?"

"I do know, Peggy. I'm just asking for whatever you heard."

"When I brought the check over, I think they were talking about maybe walking across."

"You recall who said it?"

"No. They were all talking. I thought they were nuts or maybe just kidding around. That was a crazy thing to do. These were guys with wives and families."

"Do you remember when they left?"

"Not late. Eight, eight-thirty."

"Did they drink wine with dinner or have another drink after the first?"

"You know, they didn't. That's what makes me think they were planning this hike before I heard them talking about it. Usually Clark would have another beer, Val would have a glass of wine."

"And Matty?"

"Depended. But he usually had a second drink, too. None of them drank a second that night."

"And they seemed happy and friendly when they left?"

"Oh, yeah. Just like always."

"Peggy, did you have the feeling that all three of them intended to make the hike?"

"I couldn't be sure. I didn't hear anyone say he wouldn't go, but like I told you, I didn't hear everything."

"I guess that's it," I said. "Unless you can think of anything else they said."

She thought a moment. "Nothing important. One of them said something about not having boots on. That's about it."

"Do you remember who that was?"

"I couldn't tell you."

"But you heard someone mention boots."

"Yeah, I'm pretty sure. Somebody said something about boots. It was February. There was still plenty of snow around."

"Thanks, Peggy," I said. I shook her hand and went to the bar to find Carlotta.

Carlotta drove from Giordano's to the beach and clocked it. It was five miles and took about fifteen minutes. All the streets we traveled were local, and although there was no longer any snow or ice on them, we both agreed that fifteen to twenty minutes was a fair estimate of the time.

"If the men had driven from Giordano's to any of the three houses, what would those times be?" I asked as she turned away from the beach.

"We're the closest and Clark's the farthest."

"What are we talking about in time?"

"Maybe fifteen minutes to our house, maybe half an hour to Clark's. And average the two for Matty's. What's this all about?"

"Until I talked to Peggy, I thought one of the men might just have had a gun with him at dinner. But if one of them went home to change his shoes or put snow boots on, he could have picked up a gun at the same time."

"Val didn't have a gun."

"Annie says Matty didn't own a handgun either, that all he had were hunting rifles. She was home with the kids that night, and Matty didn't come home after he left for dinner with his friends."

"So that leaves Clark."

"Or maybe one of the others had a gun that his wife didn't know about."

"And Val's the easiest target," Carlotta said. "No one was home to see him go in and out, and he lives the closest. And besides, if Matty went back for a gun, how come he ended up being the one shot?"

"I'll have to talk to Bambi. It's really very important now. I wonder if she's already told this to the police and she doesn't want to go over it again. It can't make her very happy to think that her husband killed his best friend."

"Try dropping in on her tomorrow, Chris. She'll get the kids off to school, and then maybe you can find her at home."

"Does she go into the store? You said Clark owned a hardware store."

"I think she does, but not full-time. She's got a good staff there, nice people, very trustworthy. She doesn't have to be there all the time."

"Then that's on for tomorrow. And the other person I have to talk to is Val's partner."

"I'll see what I can do."

6

At home Carlotta got a fire going in the family room, expertly laying the kindling with the heavier wood on top, starting it up with some newspaper that did its work effectively. In seconds the fireplace was ablaze, and the warmth floated to where we sat several feet away.

"That's one thing I haven't mastered," I admitted. "Jack's much better at it than I."

"I always watched Val," she said. "He had a way of placing all the different materials and sizes so that one lighted the other in sequence. I don't know where he learned how to do it, but when I came home from Oakwood, after I met you in February, I decided I didn't want to live without my evening fires. I'm not as good as Val, but the fire reminds me of him in a very happy way. That day we met on the ski slopes, in the evening we sat in front of a fire in a huge stone fireplace. It was so hot we had to move away from it."

I watched her as she spoke, her eyes on the fire, her cheeks just slightly pink. The cool, somewhat crisp facade of the businesswoman had melted away and the distraught wife—or widow—was plainly visible.

"You must be very observant. You do it so well."

"You think he's dead, don't you?" She turned to me. "You think his body's stuck at the bottom of the lake."

"I think it's very likely. But that doesn't mean I won't give it my all."

"If I could just think of where he would go. I sat and made a list one night."

"What did you come up with?"

"I started with the ski resort where we met. I know that sounds foolishly sentimental, but I thought maybe he would go there because we'd been so happy that first weekend—and there were other weekends later. But he had no money, Chris, except for what he had in his pocket."

"How much could that have been?"

"Several hundred. Maybe more. Enough to get on a plane, to buy some food, to get some new clothes. But what happened after that?" She looked at me as though she expected me to find an answer.

"He would have gone to a friend or relative," I said.

"But his friends were here, and they were dead."

"Parents?"

"Oh, they've gone."

"Dead?"

"No. They went back to Europe before I met Val."

"Were they at your wedding?"

"They weren't able to come."

"Were they Russian?"

"Actually, no. Well, I guess they were originally, or the family was. But they were German."

"I see. So you've never met them."

"No."

"Did they keep in touch?"

"Not really." She looked uncomfortable. "I don't really know—Val didn't talk about them much."

"Were they from the east or the west?"

"The east."

"Did he grow up there?"

"No, he was born here."

"I would think after the Berlin Wall came down they wouldn't have had much trouble coming over, especially with a son living here, an American-born son."

"I really don't know, Chris. I assume there was something between Val and his parents that he didn't tell me about. I see from your face that you think this is very strange and you're right, but I've told you what I know." As though to change the subject, she reached for a crystal bowl full of candy and passed it to me. "Have a mint. I always like one after dinner."

"Thank you."

"It's not alcoholic, so you don't have to worry." She smiled.

"Then I'll take two. I have a sweet tooth."

"You don't look it. You must do a lot of exercise."

"Haphazardly at best. I walk in the morning. I'm an early riser, and I can get out and back in time to have breakfast with Jack before he leaves for Brooklyn."

"Val and I always had breakfast together."

"Let's get back to your list. What other places did you think Val might go to?"

"One obvious person is his partner. They've known each other a long time, and they trust each other. I've talked to Jake frequently since Val's disappearance, but he swears he hasn't seen Val since Valentine's Day."

"Has he heard from him?"

"He says no. As everyone else does."

"Well, he's high on my list, so let's see what we can do there. I have another question. It's a subject I don't like to talk about, but what I found in his desk has made me wonder. Do the two of you have wills?"

"I don't. I've never thought about it. I assume Val doesn't either. He never told me he did."

"Do you have a lawyer?"

"No. We've never needed one. If we did, I'd ask around and get a recommendation. Come to think of it, Val must know a lawyer. He's in a partnership in his business. They must have some legal agreement, don't you think?"

"That's very likely. And if he used that lawyer to set up his business, he might use him to write a will."

"Why are you asking about this?"

"Because there's a lot of money, Carlotta, almost three hundred thousand dollars in those three books. For all we know there could be more. He may have stock certificates in a safe deposit box. The thing that struck me was that all three accounts were in his name alone. None of them were joint accounts or in trust for you—or for anyone else. I would think that someone with that much money would have a will directing where it should go."

"I'm his wife. Wouldn't I inherit if he died?"

"Probably. It just seems a little strange. I don't know a lot about these things, but Jack and I have a joint checking account, and when we got married, we made all our savings accounts either joint or in trust for the other."

"Our checking account is joint, and we have a joint savings account at a local bank."

"Besides those three in his desk."

"Yes."

"Did you know about those accounts?"

She took a moment to answer. "I knew he had other accounts. He told me a long time ago there were bankbooks in his desk. I never saw them till after he disappeared."

"Were you surprised at how much money there was?"

"Maybe a little. We never talked about money, Chris. When we wanted to buy something, like the house, Val would say we could afford it or he didn't think we could afford it. He knew what I was earning, and I had a pretty good idea of what he was earning. I just didn't think about it. And we never talked about writing wills."

"Do you have a safe deposit box?"

"Yes. It's in both our names. Want to go down there tomorrow and see what's there?"

"If you don't mind."

"How's nine A.M.?"

"It's good for me."

"Me, too. I'll set my alarm for seven-thirty."

"Fine. We'll take it from there."

We got to the bank just as it was opening, and as Carlotta signed the card, it seemed to occur to both of us at the same moment that this was something to check. She got the assistant manager to go through the records to see whether Val had accessed the box any time after February fourteenth. The search took only a few minutes, and the answer was no. The last time anyone had used the box was in January, and it had been Carlotta.

We went back together to the boxes. The one Carlotta pulled out of the slot was larger than the one I had inherited from Aunt Meg and now owned jointly with Jack. We took it into a small room with a single chair and a door that closed and locked.

Carlotta opened the box and started through the papers. "I keep some jewelry here," she said as she looked. "Stuff I don't wear often. Here are some automobile papers, our marriage certificate. What's this?" She pulled out an envelope and looked inside. "This looks like papers for Val's business. And the envelope has the lawyer's name and address on it."

"Let's write it down. We may want to talk to him."

She continued through the papers. "Here's Val's birth certificate. He was born in Connecticut." She handed it to me. "And here's the deed to the house."

I wrote down the information on the birth certificate, glanced at the deed, and asked her if there was anything else that looked important.

"I can't find anything."

"So there's nothing that looks like a will."

"Nothing at all. You want to have a look?"

"No, that's fine."

"Then that's it. No, here's something I missed. It's from an insurance company." She pulled out an envelope and looked inside. "It's a life insurance policy. I never knew Val carried any. My God, Chris, it's a million dollars on his life."

"Who's the beneficiary?"

She looked pale. "I can't believe this. Matty is. Matthew Franklin." She looked at me, her face asking the question she could barely articulate. "Why would he do this, Chris? Val's left a million dollars to Matty. A million dollars."

I wondered if she was thinking that he hadn't left anything like that to her.

* * *

She was somber on the way home. The envelopes with the insurance policy and the business papers lay on the seat between us.

"You don't think there were any other insurance policies in the box besides this one?" I asked.

"There weren't. I looked."

"We'll have to find out if there's a will."

"Wouldn't he keep that in the box?"

"Maybe it's with an attorney."

"I've never felt so confused in my life."

"I know you're thinking that this makes it look as though Val had a motive for killing Matty, but it doesn't. He could have cancelled that policy at any time, or changed the beneficiary. Maybe he took it out before you were married and he forgot about it."

"How do you forget about a million dollars?"

I was asking myself the same thing. "He may have stopped paying the premiums, Carlotta. Anyway, whether Val is dead or alive, he isn't legally dead so no one's going to inherit that insurance."

"I hadn't thought of that."

"And I'm sure I don't have to tell you that Annie Franklin doesn't have to know about it."

"She certainly won't hear it from me."

"And maybe we'll turn up a reason."

"I'd rather turn up a husband." She turned quickly toward me and gave me a fleeting smile. "If it's all the same to you."

7

I left Carlotta in Val's study, going through his desk drawers to see if she could find the answers to the disturbing questions we had just unearthed. As I drove toward Bambi Thayer's house I wondered whether the insurance policy could have lapsed, whether Val had taken it out years ago and then stopped paying the premiums on it, perhaps when he married. It had been the bottom envelope in the box, indicating that it might be the oldest. I would have to check when I got back.

Bambi's house was more modest than Annie's, but well cared-for, lots of shrubs planted near the front of the house and handsome specimen trees on the front lawn. I parked at the curb. A car was in the driveway and the garage door was open.

I was a little nervous as I walked up to the front door. Bambi didn't want to see me, and she might exercise her right not to invite me in and talk to me. I didn't look forward to a confrontation and hoped there wouldn't be one.

The door opened after the first ring. The young woman who stood just inside was slim, with lots of curly dark blond hair, and pale skin. She wore no makeup and was dressed in jeans and a long-sleeved shirt with the sleeves rolled up.

"Yes?"

"Mrs. Thayer, I'm Chris Bennett."

"Who?"

"I'm looking into the disappearance of Val Krassky."

"Oh, you. I told Carlotta I didn't want to talk to you. Didn't you get the message?"

"I did and I'm sorry to intrude, but I thought if you had a few minutes—I don't want to upset you, but I think you know a lot that can be helpful."

She gave me an appraising look, her face tight and her eyes cool. "You're not what I expected."

I didn't know how to respond, so I said nothing.

"Come on in." She opened the door all the way, and I walked into her foyer. "Give me your coat. We can sit in the living room. I've just been picking up after the kids." She hung my coat in a closet next to the door, and we went into the living room and sat.

"I appreciate this," I said.

"I expected some tough detective-type."

"I teach a course in poetry at a college near my home."

"Poetry," she said, as though it were something she hadn't heard about for a long time. "My dad used to read poetry."

"Bambi, I'm very sorry about your husband."

Her eyes filled with tears. "They were crazy to go out on the lake that night. They should have known better— Clark should have known better. He could never say no when Matty dared him, but he didn't kill Matty. He loved him. I don't care what Annie and Carlotta say. Clark didn't have it in him to kill anything."

"When did you last see Clark?"

"Sometime that afternoon. It was Val's birthday and

the guys were going out to celebrate. They went to this Italian restaurant they liked."

"What did he say before he left?"

"Not to wait up for him."

"Was that unusual?"

She shook her head. "Not when the three of them went out together. Sometimes they'd take in a late movie, sometimes they'd go to a bar and sit for a couple of hours. I didn't think anything of it. He said good-bye to the kids and kissed me—" She swallowed painfully.

"Did he come back to the house for anything later?"

"No. He walked out and I never saw him again."

"Were you home that night?"

"The whole night."

"Do you remember if he was wearing boots when he left the house?"

"Work boots, I think. He wore them a lot in the winter."

"Did Clark own a gun?" I asked.

"Never." She looked very defensive. "Never in his life."

"Did he sell guns in the store?"

"No. He sold hardware things, tools and nails and building and household supplies."

"How did he get into the business?" I asked. "Did he start the store himself or was it his parents'?"

"His parents are dead. He started working for the original owner when he was young. When the old guy wanted to retire, Clark bought him out. It's a real institution, that store. We've got everything."

"But no guns."

"No guns. I don't think Clark ever shot a gun in his life. Matty did. He was a big hunter. He probably had a handgun even if Annie says he didn't. Annie says what's convenient."

"What about Val? Do you think he could have owned a gun?"

"Anyone could own a gun. Since the accident, I've been thinking about getting one myself, but I'm scared because of the kids. They're into everything. A gun's no good if it's locked away when you need it."

"Did you get along with Carlotta and Annie?"

"I got along. We all got along."

"Do you like them as friends?"

"I have other friends. These were my husband's friends' wives. I liked them. Annie's been very nice to me since the accident, I mean really nice. Carlotta's been a little cool. She went away somewhere right after it happened and when she came back, I don't know. It's been tough on all of us. She's called a lot."

"I heard you had a funeral for Clark right after the accident."

"I knew they were gone," she said. "They found Matty's red scarf at the break in the ice. I knew if he was gone, then Clark was gone."

"Carlotta thinks Val is still alive," I said.

"Don't you believe it. He's gone, too. They went on that ice together and they died together. He'll float up. He'll probably have a bullet hole in him, too. Watch and see."

"Who do you think shot him?"

"Matty. I think Matty shot Val first. Then Clark got the gun away from him and shot him accidentally. That's how this all happened."

"Why would Matty shoot Val?" I asked.

"Jealousy," she said. "Matty never succeeded at

anything in his whole life. His life was one failure after another. The only thing he did right was marrying Annie. She was a catch. She's good-looking, and she's got some money. It helps, when you have a husband that doesn't always bring home a paycheck."

"How did Matty and Annie meet?" I thought it would be a good idea to get everyone's point of view.

"I think Val knew her first. He may even have introduced them. It was before Val met Carlotta."

"Was Annie from around here?"

"Uh, from near New York, I think. New Jersey, maybe."

"Do you think there was anything going on between Val and Annie?"

Her eyebrows rose. "Val and Annie? I never thought of that."

"Think about it now."

She looked at me. Her face was so serious through the whole conversation that she could have been working through a final exam. "I don't think so," she said. "Val and Carlotta, they're a good couple. They're good together. And I think Matty and Annie were, too. Annie likes to flirt a little, but I don't think she means anything by it. She's got a real good heart."

It was hard to tell whether Bambi was being honest or saying nice things because she thought it was the right thing to do. She struck me as a genuinely good person— but I've been wrong before.

"Does Clark have brothers and sisters?"

"No, there's just him. Maybe that's why he always felt the guys were like his brothers. A person needs a family. I've got a big one, and it's helped a lot, especially since the accident."

"Bambi, when did the three men become friends?"

"It must have been at Bennett High School. That's in Buffalo. It couldn't have been later. Val went off to one college and Matty went to another. Clark went to UB for a semester and then dropped out. So if they hadn't known each other in high school, they would never have met. They were all in different places after that."

"So they all went to Bennett?"

"I think so. Clark did. He told me."

"Was he living with his parents then?"

"He must have been. I'm not sure when they died, but I don't think it was that long ago. I mean, he was finished with school by that time."

"Bambi, I'm staying with Carlotta. You can call me there if you want to tell me anything. If you don't want her to know you've called, I'll give you my phone number at home. Leave a message on my answering machine or tell my husband, Jack, you want to talk to me."

"OK."

I wrote the number and my name on a slip of paper and gave it to her. "If Val wanted to disappear, do you have any idea where he would go?"

"Val's dead, Chris. You don't walk away from an accident on the ice. Don't you know what that red scarf meant? Clark was pulling Matty up with it after Matty was shot. The double weight must have broken the ice under Clark, and he dropped in the water, too. Matty must have let go of the scarf. That's how come they found it. It was very light, cashmere or something. But they all went down. You're not going to find Val alive. It's all over."

I thanked her for her time and her help and drove back to Carlotta's house, mulling over her theory of the scarf.

* * *

Carlotta was sitting in a leather chair in Val's study, three desk drawers stacked beside her. She looked up as I entered the room. "Success?" she said.

"Yes. She talked to me. She thinks Matty was the man with the gun."

"If I had to guess, I'd say the same thing. So she thinks Clark took the gun away from him?"

"In a fight that started between Matty and Val."

"Over what?"

"Jealousy. Val had everything, Matty couldn't make it in the world of business."

"She's got it right there, but Matty never seemed jealous of anyone. Quite the reverse."

"It's just a theory. Have you found anything in the desk?"

"Nothing to explain that insurance policy. But I've learned something very interesting. I called the company and tried to find out whether the policy was still active. The agent gave me a little lesson in insurance. If Matty died before Val, no one inherits the million. And if both of them died in the accident, before Annie could inherit there would have to be proof that Val died first."

"That is interesting. So if Val is alive, Annie doesn't inherit. And even if Val's body is found, it's a tough case to prove."

"Exactly." I noted a little triumph in her voice.

"Is there a date on the policy, Carlotta?" I sat in the other leather chair.

"Yes. He took it out about a year before I met him."

"Maybe Matty was in financial trouble and Val wanted to see to it that he was taken care of."

"Maybe," she said, but it was clear she wasn't convinced.

"Carlotta, what we've learned in the last few hours is that there was something unusual about the relationship those three men had. Each of the wives has told me that her husband loved the other two, but Bambi thought Matty was jealous of Val, and Annie thought there was bad blood between Val and Matty because of her."

"That's absurd."

"It doesn't matter whether it's absurd. It doesn't even matter whether it's true. They have these perceptions. You seem to be the only one of the three who doesn't feel there was trouble between any two of them."

"There wasn't. They were friends, they loved each other, they went out together and we went out as couples. Annie and Bambi are looking for something where nothing exists. I understand why. They've lost their husbands—and maybe I have, too, but I think when they were having dinner that night at Giordano's, they were three happy guys."

"One of whom had a gun."

She didn't answer. She looked down at the drawer next to her and pulled out a couple of pieces of paper. "I certainly haven't found a license to carry a gun here."

"Bambi was home the whole night on February fourteenth. She says Clark never came back after he left for dinner. He was wearing work boots when he went out."

"He always did in the winter," Carlotta said. "He would have to go outside with a customer to pick something up or put it in the car." Her voice was low. Only her husband had no one to vouch for him.

* * *

I sat in the living room and looked at the local paper. There's nothing stranger than reading the problems of a community about which you know nothing. The names make no sense, the problems, while often similar to hometown problems, have their own peculiar spins. Carlotta had said the *New York Times* would not be available till about noon; they were flown in from New York and then had to be driven from the airport. You forget sometimes how much you get used to living in the New York metropolitan area.

I had walked out of the study to leave her alone. She had invited me here to try to find her husband, and everything I had learned made it seem that he was the man with the gun. I put the paper down and thought about who else I needed to find and talk to. Jake, Val's business partner, was at the top of the list, and every time I had mentioned him, Carlotta had rather deftly turned the conversation away from him. It might not hurt to talk to the detective in charge of the case, too. He would know whether any taxi drivers remembered driving Val away from the beach that night, and maybe he would have tried to find the bus drivers, too, although that was surely a slim possibility. So there was Jake and there was the detective. And after that, there was the inevitable question: Then, what? It's the question I hate most.

I put my forehead in my hand, closed my eyes, and tried to see where all this was leading. Val had no family to turn to, so where would he go? But he did have a family, parents who lived somewhere in Germany. Could he have left the country?

"Sorry I fell apart, Chris." Carlotta's voice came from behind.

"Carlotta, did Val have a passport?" I stood, suddenly filled with renewed energy.

"Yes, we both did."

"Where did he keep it? It wasn't in the safe deposit box."

"You're right. Let me think. He kept both our passports. We went to England and France last year, so they're new. They must be in his chest of drawers. You didn't find them in the desk, did you?"

"No. I would have looked at his."

"You think he left the country?"

"I don't know what to think. But he has parents over there. Even if they weren't on good terms, when you're in trouble, you go home."

"Come upstairs with me. I'll look in the chest."

I followed her up to her bedroom, a large room with an adjoining sitting room and bath, the kind of luxury that takes my breath away. She went directly to a large chest of drawers and opened the top drawer.

"He keeps certain personal papers here," she said. "I've never looked before, but I remember he took the passports out of this drawer before we went away. Let's see, I think they're dark blue."

I stood away from her, not wanting to interfere. If nothing turned up pretty soon, I would have to ask her permission to go through the contents myself.

"Here they are, two passports, his and hers." She handed them to me.

I opened Val's and looked at the first few pages, at the picture, then at the stamps from English and French immigration, and finally from the U.S. at the end of their trip. "I guess he didn't leave the country," I said, somewhat disappointed. Not that I could have located his parents even if I could prove he had flown to Germany.

"And everything here is pretty neat," she said. "It doesn't look disrupted, as if he were looking for something in a hurry."

"Were there ever any calls to Germany on your phone bill?"

"Never. I would remember that."

"Any other foreign country?"

"We don't have friends there. I don't even know how to dial Europe."

"Then that pretty much leaves that out. There are two people I want to see, Carlotta, Jake and the detective in charge of the case. Do you think you can get me to see one of them this afternoon?"

"I'll call the sheriff's office and see if Detective Murdock is there. He might come down to our local police station, and we can go over after lunch."

"And Jake?"

"I'll call him later." She looked at her watch. "It's time for lunch. We have a nice little coffee shop in the center of town, and I haven't been there since they renovated. Want to give it a try?"

I said I did, but I really wanted to know why she wouldn't call her husband's partner and set up a meeting.

8

The coffee shop had been transformed into a tearoom in the time since Carlotta had last visited, and it was very pretty, with flowered wallpaper, little round tables with fussy cloths, and a scalloped menu offering appealing things to eat. Before leaving the house Carlotta had set up an appointment with Detective Murdock, and when we finished our dainty lunch we walked down the street to the police station. It was the kind of homey place that Oakwood's police station is, where people are greeted in a friendly way and treated like neighbors. I remembered with some amusement the first time I went to the Brooklyn station house where I met Jack and talked to a desk sergeant, a woman who begrudged me the thirty seconds it took to tell me she couldn't help me because the case was too old. I had the feeling this was a place where, even if the message were the same, the delivery would be a lot more pleasant.

Detective Murdock came down a hall and shook hands with Carlotta. He was tall and had a deep voice, a thick mustache, and a trimmer body than a lot of Jack's fellow cops.

"Detective, this is Chris Bennett, a friend from near New York City. She's trying to help me find Val."

"Good to meet you," he said, extending a large hand, which I shook. "You want to know what I know?"

"If you'll tell me."

"Sure. Want to come this way?"

"I'll see you later," Carlotta said, and I walked along beside Murdock, entering a small office with a desk and two chairs.

"Take your coat off and make yourself comfortable. I know what you're here for. Mrs. Krassky told me about it. She thinks her husband's still alive, doesn't she?"

"She hopes he is."

"Well, we all hope he is, we just don't think it's possible."

"May I sketch out a couple of ways I think he might be alive?"

"It's all yours. I'd love to hear them."

"One is that he never went to the lake with his friends on the night of Valentine's Day."

"You mean he went home after they all had dinner together?"

"Yes. That's what Carlotta thinks happened. She thinks her husband wouldn't have gone to the lake with the others because he wasn't the kind of person who would walk across the frozen lake."

"Are you aware his watch was found in Mr. Franklin's vehicle?"

I was and it troubled me. "Maybe he changed his mind after he took the watch off."

The detective smiled. "A little far out, but stranger things have happened. If he didn't go, I'll grant you he may be alive. The question is, where is he. And another important question is why he's in hiding."

"I don't know where, Detective. But I think the why is

fairly obvious. He goes home, he goes to sleep, he gets up in the morning expecting to go to work, and he hears the news of his friends' disappearance."

"That news didn't break early in the morning."

That was exactly what I had told Carlotta. "Maybe he'd had a tough night, and he decided to sleep in. He didn't report to anyone at work; he was a principal. His wife wasn't home; he didn't have to get up for breakfast. By the time he got up, the news may have broken."

"What about the two other wives? They told me they called Mr. Krassky's home to see if he'd come in."

"Were there messages on the answering machine?"

"As a matter of fact, yes. Mrs. Thayer left a message. Mrs. Franklin said she hung up before the machine picked up. Said she knew it would kick in after the fourth ring."

"He may have been home and wasn't answering the phone. Lots of people do that."

"With his wife away? Would he chance missing a call from her?"

"If he heard her voice, he could always pick up."

He smiled again. "OK, you got me. Keep going."

"Here's the second possibility. He followed his two friends across the lake. Maybe he was the laggard. From a distance he could have seen the argument between the other two men, or heard the shot, and retreated to save his own life."

"I'll give you points for that. He gets tired, he thinks maybe he shouldn't have come this far, and then the argument happens and he runs for his life."

"If that's what happened," I said, "he probably saw and heard them go down. And he had a long way to go back to the beach, from where I've heard the break in the ice was."

"Seven or eight miles," he agreed. "Couple hours at a good pace. Now you're going to tell me he was distraught and confused and could think of nothing else but getting the hell out of town, hiding from reality, all that good stuff."

"I think it could have happened."

"What could also have happened is that he was the man with the gun, he pulled the trigger, one man went down, the other went to help, both went through the ice, and Valentine Krassky is a fugitive from justice."

"But if he carried the gun, Detective Murdock, with the intention of shooting Matty Franklin, why would he leave his watch in the car?" Watching his face, I felt rather triumphant.

"Good point," the detective said, picking up a pen and making a note for the first time.

"And even if what you suggested is true, he could be alive. And that would be a good reason why he didn't let anyone know where he was."

"We're working on that angle. He's on our wanted list. Just in case his body doesn't turn up hooked to the branch of an underwater tree."

"Did you check the taxi companies?" I asked.

"You have to understand, when this tragedy happened, we assumed all three men were together—we had no reason to assume otherwise—so we didn't look elsewhere for any of them. That left us kinda behind when only two bodies surfaced and we realized there'd been a shoot-out. But yes, I've checked the taxi companies in the area, and no one remembers picking anyone up that night that could have been Mr. Krassky. And this tragedy has been in the news, Ms. Bennett. If a driver had picked up one of those missing men, you can bet he would have come forward on his own."

"Unless he'd been paid to keep quiet."

"But then we've got a fugitive, and that's not what Mrs. Krassky is hoping for."

"What about buses?" I asked, not wanting to get off on a tangent.

"I talked to the bus company myself. If anyone fitting Mr. Krassky's description took a bus that night, none of the drivers remembers it."

"Which doesn't mean he didn't."

"Doesn't mean a damn thing."

"Could he have walked home from the beach?"

"Sure. Take awhile, but it's easier going than on ice."

We had driven it in fifteen minutes and clocked it at five miles. I can walk three miles in an hour without pushing myself. "The question really is, where would he go? He didn't leave the country because we found his passport this morning."

The detective smiled. "And he didn't take any money out of the bank. At least not that we know of. Don't forget, he may have had an account somewhere else, like in another state, that we don't know about. And for all we know, he hopped on a bus to that place, where he's stashed a bundle and started a new life right there. Or anywhere else you can think of."

"If that's true, he might have gone to a place where he has friends his wife doesn't know about."

Murdock gave me a sly smile. "Now you're thinking the way cops think."

"I'll have to look at Carlotta's phone bills and see who he called."

"That's a start." The way he spoke, it was clear he didn't think there was a chance in a million that Val was alive. He was just gone, and everything I was doing was a waste of time.

"There were no sightings that you've heard about?" I said.

"Not a one. Of course, as I said before, we didn't start looking till last week because we thought they all died together in February. It leaves us with a pretty cold trail."

No sightings, no taxis, no buses, no wife at home. "Neighbors?" I asked.

"The neighbors said they were a nice couple. Some of them were very friendly with the Krasskys, had dinner with them, visited each others' homes. If he came home the morning of the fifteenth or left his home that day, no one saw him."

"Which doesn't mean it didn't happen."

"Doesn't mean it didn't happen, but there's been nothing, Ms. Bennett. You're trying to convince me that this man is alive, that he left his watch behind but didn't walk across the lake, that he's living somewhere without benefit of his life savings, that he's never called the wife he loves, and even that he had no hand in the shooting. Do you see where I'm going?"

"Pretty low probability," I said, feeling the weight of all that negative evidence.

"Probability zero. I don't want to hurt your feelings, but I think you're wasting your time. Even more so, because if he's alive, he's a killer. And that's not what Mrs. Krassky wants."

"No, it's the last thing she wants." I stood. There didn't seem to be much else we could talk about.

Detective Murdock took a card out of his pocket and

handed it to me. "If you get a lead out of state or anywhere else, will you let me know?"

"Of course."

"You look kinda down. I'm sorry."

"It's OK. It's what I've thought all along, but I wanted
to believe there was some hope."

"There isn't any. Believe me."

I had to admit I believed him.

I walked outside the police station and stood in the
bright sunlight, shading my eyes and looking up and
down the street for Carlotta. She wasn't around, and I
walked tentatively down the street and looked in shop
windows. There was a lovely store that sold cooking
equipment. My friend Melanie Gross would have to
restrain herself here. Gleaming stainless steel pots and
pans were the least of it. There were gadgets that looked
as though they would accomplish every drudgery-filled
task of cooking and baking, barbecue utensils that would
make my life—and Jack's—a lot easier, spices and mus-
tards, and serving platters that looked hand-painted. I
decided this was not the place to wait for Carlotta, and
I must not go inside under any conditions. Fortunately, I
have refused firmly to carry a credit card, much to Jack's
displeasure. He is a man who always thinks of emergen-
cies, and although I know he is right, I don't ever want to
succumb to temptation.

"Done already?"

I turned and there was Carlotta, a bakery bag in her
hand. "Done, and resisting temptation with difficulty."

"I suspect you're a person who resists a lot more easily
than most people."

I wasn't sure if that was a compliment. "Depends on the temptation," I said.

"What did you learn?"

"Nothing about the case that we didn't already know or assume. Murdock himself checked the taxi companies and buses, and no one remembers seeing Val on the four-teenth and fifteenth."

"Which doesn't mean he didn't take one."

"He understands that, Carlotta. It's just that everything is a negative, and to believe that Val is alive, you have to reject all these negative indications."

"I'm sorry. Go on."

"When I suggested that Val never made the lake crossing, he pointed out that the watch was found in Matty's car. He also told me that Bambi left a message on your answering machine the morning of the fifteenth."

"I didn't remember that. I guess I was in a fog when I got back from my trip." She looked troubled. We started walking down the block to where we had left the car. "But there wasn't one from Annie, was there?"

"Murdock suggested Val might have had money stashed in another state where he might also have friends you didn't know about. Do you have your phone bills from the last few months? I'd like to see what the long distance calls look like."

"I have everything." She unlocked the car door for me and went around to the other side. "I don't see those bills very often, but if I make business calls from home, I keep a list of them for reimbursement," she said, when we were both in the car. "Sometimes Val makes business calls from home, too, and I know he does business with out-of-state people. You can call all the numbers on the bills if you want."

"I may do that." We drove away from the main street and toward the residential part of town, which was a short walk from there. "Have you called Val's partner yet?" I asked.

"I will when we get home."

In Val's study Carlotta pulled out a tax file with this year's gas, electric, and telephone bills. Since Val had disappeared early in the year, she found the file for last year and gave it to me. I sat at his desk and started with February, working back. The phone bills were many pages long, with a lot of toll calls to the 716 area and others to places as far away as California. Before I started, Carlotta warned me that she called old friends who were now scattered around the country, and she also called her parents regularly. She jotted down several of those numbers so I wouldn't have to ask about them later.

This was the kind of work that real police detectives often spend their time doing, while those on TV are out in the middle of the night with their guns blazing. It wasn't any more interesting for me than it was for Jack and his fellow detectives, and I had to keep myself from nodding off once or twice.

I skipped over the known friends and relatives; I could come back to them later, but Carlotta didn't seem to think Val would be hiding out with her parents or her high school chums. Her parents, in particular, would have a hard time keeping his presence a secret from their daughter, and Val hadn't known most of her old friends, who lived out-of-state. One number that appeared repeat- edly was Amy Grant's in Oakwood, and if Val were there, Amy had done a masterful job of keeping him away from Carlotta while Carlotta was visiting.

I noticed that in the bills preceding February, certain telephone numbers were checked in red ink, and Carlotta told me that those were Val's business calls made from home. Every out-of-state number that she didn't recognize was checked.

I went back a full year, yawning by the time I decided to call it quits. Carlotta was sitting in the family room reading when I found her.

"Anything?" she said.

"All the out-of-state numbers that aren't on your list were checked by Val."

"Then they're business. Call them if you want, Chris. But I don't think they'll lead anywhere."

"Before I do that, there's something else I'd like to try. I copied down the address of Val's parents from his birth certificate. I know it's a long time ago, but many people do stay in one place. I'd just like to see if there's a number for them."

"I can assure you they're not in the country."

"Humor me."

She smiled. "You sound like me at work. OK, I'll humor you. Give it a try."

She followed me to the kitchen, where I called Connecticut information and asked for the number of Gregory Krassky at the Trumbull address.

"I have no Krassky at that address," the operator said.

"Maybe they've moved," I said. "It's awhile since I've called them."

"Let me check the name."

There was a click and then a mechanical voice came on. "That number is—" and a telephone number followed. I could hear Carlotta gasp as she saw me write it down. I hung up and looked at her.

"There's a number for that name?" she said.

"In the same town. At least in the same directory."

Her hand pressed against her chest. "This isn't possible."

I picked up the phone and dialed, my own heart doing funny things.

"Hello?" It was a woman's voice.

"Mrs. Krassky?"

"Yes. Who's this?"

"My name is Christine Bennett, Mrs. Krassky. I'm a friend of your son, Val."

"Who is this?" she said angrily.

"I'm a friend of Val's," I said as calmly as I could manage. "I wanted to ask—"

"What kind of joke is this?" the woman said with anguish. "My son is dead. Val is dead. Leave me alone." And she hung up.

I hung up, too, and looked at Carlotta who was standing near me, transfixed. "I think I've found them," I said. "I just spoke to Val's mother."

9

We sat in the breakfast room and talked about it, Carlotta sipping a cup of tea, which I would have loved to have. I drank a glass of skim milk instead, not enjoying it very much but knowing I was doing the right thing.

"How does she know he died? Do you think someone sent her the newspaper clippings?" Carlotta said. "I can't believe a Connecticut paper would have run the story, and even if they had, they wouldn't have mentioned the names of the three men. No one there would be likely to know them."

"I don't know," I said. "Something's really bothering me about what that woman said. I just can't put my finger on it."

"Why wouldn't Val tell me they were there? Even if something happened in their relationship, if they had a disagreement, why would he concoct a story about their returning to Europe?"

"Something's wrong, Carlotta." We seemed to be holding separate monologues, neither of us listening to the other. "Why can't I put my finger on what it is?"

"Somebody here in western New York called the Krasskys and told them Val was dead. But they don't know any more than the police do. It doesn't mean he's dead, Chris. It just means Mrs. Krassky thinks he is."

"Everything she said was wrong." I took a last gulp of milk, happy that I had downed my quarter-quart for the afternoon.

"It means he didn't go there," Carlotta said. "We can scratch Connecticut as a safe haven. He's somewhere else."

"Carlotta, listen to me. Have you ever called the family of someone who died to deliver your condolences?"

"Yes, a few times."

"So have I. What was their reaction?"

"They were touched. They were often deeply moved that I had called."

"Exactly. That's been the reaction I got, too."

"I see what you mean. You said she was angry."

"She was spitting mad. She said, 'What kind of joke is this?' Who would ever say that if you were a friend of the deceased and had taken the time and trouble to call?"

"What does that mean?" She looked thoroughly confused.

"I'm not sure."

"Maybe they're not his parents."

"There may be another explanation." I looked at my watch. "Let's wait till seven or eight tonight. Then you call, so if Mrs. Krassky picks up, she won't recognize the voice. Ask to talk to her husband. Let's work out a script before you call. Maybe you can get something from the father."

"Like what?"

"I wish I knew."

* * *

"Let's consider the possibilities," I said. We had driven to a restaurant known for its seafood, and Carlotta had insisted I order lobster. I told her I had only eaten it once before in my life and I wasn't very adept at cracking the shell and extracting the meat, but she promised to assist and I relented. Lobster was the kind of treat that might not come my way again very soon.

"One is it's a mistake," Carlotta said, starting out with the most optimistic point of view. "We called the wrong people."

"Let's look at the more realistic side. A number of years ago, before you met him, Val and his parents had a parting of the ways. Some kind of rift developed that couldn't be patched up. They parted and each side told a different story; Val said his parents had returned to Europe, which is where they came from; his parents decided they had lost him so completely that he was as good as dead."

"And they're still pained by the memory of whatever happened between them. Maybe they've even come to believe it," Carlotta said. "That their son died."

"Maybe." I was a lot less anxious to embrace one of my hypotheticals than she was. I was looking for truth; Carlotta was looking for a living husband.

"The woman you talked to, did she have an accent?"

"No, she didn't, which is another thing that's bothersome."

"It means Val lied about their coming from Europe. But I can see that. He didn't want me to think they were in the country, so he fabricated the whole story about where they came from."

"Let's leave that one and move on. Let's say these

people in Connecticut believe their son died, but he didn't."

"I don't see that. You can believe someone you haven't seen in a long time has died, someone who lives far away, but your own child?"

"I'm thinking wild thoughts. Maybe he was kidnapped as a child."

She thought about it, but I could see she didn't like it any more than I did. "It doesn't make sense. If he knew his name, he would know where to find his parents. He had the birth certificate, Chris. He knew where he came from. If he'd been snatched as a baby, his name would have been changed. If you snatched a baby, you'd call it Something Brooks, wouldn't you?"

"OK, I admit that's not very good."

The lobsters came at that point, and we put our bibs on and got to work, but I couldn't stop thinking about it. The woman had been angry. She thought I was playing a nasty joke on her. In her mind, her son was dead. "How about this?" I said, setting my nutcracker aside for a moment. "Two boys are in an old shack and it burns to the ground. One of them is burned to death; the other escapes. The Krasskys believe the body is that of their son."

She thought about it, her face deep in concentration. "Don't they use dental records in cases like that?"

"Maybe only one boy was thought to be in the building, and that was Val. Maybe the boys were young, eight or ten years old, and they hadn't had dental work yet."

"Val has good teeth," she said slowly. "He goes for checkups, but he rarely has a cavity. I'm not sure, but he may even have all his wisdom teeth." I could see she was on the verge of accepting my new theory. "But why didn't he go home after the fire or the accident or whatever it was?"

I was ready for that one. "Two possibilities: one, he set the fire; two, he didn't get along with his parents. This was his opportunity to run away. For all we know, he created the opportunity."

She shuddered. "How did he survive in the adult world? Eight or ten years old—you have to be pretty streetwise to make it."

"Twelve," I suggested, "fourteen, sixteen."

"Yes."

"A boy who has good teeth and rarely sees a dentist, and a boy who's homeless and has never seen one."

"My God. Chris, we have to see these people." She looked at her watch. "I can probably get us on a plane tomorrow if I call tonight."

"Carlotta, this is just a theory. Let's not dash out to Connecticut. Let's call tonight and then decide what to do."

"Isn't it better to talk to people face-to-face? We're two very nonthreatening women. If they look at us, they'll feel at ease."

She was right about that. I admit to feeling frequently uneasy on the phone, not knowing whom I'm talking to or what they look like. But to assume with no hard evidence that my little scenario was the right one was too much of a stretch. "Let's call. We can always fly out there afterwards if we decide we have to. We'll still look nonthreatening when they open the door."

"All right. But I think you've put your finger on what happened. I think there was some kind of accident, and then he ran away and fabricated the story of his parents' going back to Europe. In a way, it's a combination of two of your theories." She was quietly excited, hardly eating now. "I sensed there was something strange, something different about his early life. He was never clear about his parents, about why they went back. He never talked about his childhood. I talked about mine. I had good parents, a good family, a nice house to live in, a great school, wonderful friends." She looked at me. "Val didn't. I knew that, but I only knew it in a general way because he never talked about it. I wonder what these people are like."

"We'll find out, Carlotta. Let me put together some questions for Mr. Krassky. Do you have a speakerphone in the house?"

"The one in Val's study has one. We can call from there." She put her fork down. "I don't think I can eat any more."

"Calm down. This is so good, it's a shame to waste it."

She gave me a small smile. "You're right. It's just that I'm starting to feel that we're getting somewhere. I know we haven't found him, but a veil has lifted. Do you think—is it possible that the bullet in Matty is somehow connected to Val's childhood?"

"I have no idea. Maybe after you talk to Gregory Krassky tonight, we'll know a little more."

She closed her eyes. "I hope I don't blow it."

We got home about eight and sat in the study looking over the questions I had scribbled during my lobster dinner. I had no idea, of course, if Gregory Krassky was alive, but I thought it would be better for Carlotta to try to speak to him rather than to his wife, who was already upset at my call this afternoon. The one thing I was now pretty certain of was that their son, whoever he was, had not died in the recent past. He had died or disappeared or gone away some time ago, so that telling this woman that I was a friend had struck a dissonant chord.

"I don't know if I can do this," Carlotta said, sitting next to the phone with the sheet of questions on the desk in front of her.

"Whatever happens, try to stay very calm and sound very pleasant. If we decide to go there, I don't want them to throw us out at the door."

"Here goes." She pressed the speaker button and a loud dial tone filled the room. Then she dialed, each beep piercing the silence. The connection was made and the distant phone began to ring, all the sounds magnified as though under some kind of tonal microscope.

"Hello?" It was the woman.

"May I speak to Mr. Krassky, please?"

"Just a minute." The woman laid the phone down and we heard her call, "Greg? Can you pick up?"

"Hello?" It was a man's voice.

Carlotta turned and looked at me. Her face had lost its usual self-assurance, and for a moment I thought she might really come apart. But she turned to the desk, glanced at my hand-written lines, and said, "Mr. Krassky, I live near Buffalo, New York. I found your name and address recently, and I think you can help me with a problem."

"Who did you say you were?"

"My name is Carlotta French. I believe you had a son named Valentine."

"Are you the woman who called this afternoon and spoke with my wife?"

"No, I'm not, sir. I understand your son died some time ago."

"It's almost thirty years. What is your interest in his death?"

Thirty years would make him about five or six, I thought. And there went my beautiful theory up in smoke.

"I have known a man with your son's name," Carlotta said, being careful not to disclose the relationship.

"Then it's a coincidence. My son is dead. I don't see what this has to do with me."

"Can you tell me how your son died?"

We heard his breath in the room we were sitting in. "He died in a hospital," he said wearily, as though the death had occurred so recently that he had not had time to get over the newness of it.

"In a hospital? Was he in an accident?"

"It wasn't an accident. He got sick and we brought him in. We thought he was getting better, but he died in the middle of the night. What does this have to do with you?"

"Maybe it is a coincidence," Carlotta said with an echo of defeat. "Can you tell me the name of the hospital he died in?"

"This is absurd. If you have questions, write me a letter and identify yourself. I don't know what you're after, but I'm not saying anything else over the phone. And please don't call my wife. It's too upsetting for her. We lost our beautiful little son and our lives haven't been the same since. Good night, Miss French."

The hang-up crackled in our room, and Carlotta pressed the speaker button again. "I didn't get much," she said.

"You got plenty. You know when and where he died—or when he is supposed to have died. If a child's sick, you take it to the nearest hospital. I think we could look at a map and find the right one. I have another idea. Maybe another Krassky lived in that town, Gregory's brother. Maybe both men had sons with the same name."

"Two boys born on Valentine's Day?"

"Valentin is a Slavic name. It could be a family name. Maybe Val got the wrong birth certificate and never noticed it. Or maybe he just didn't want to bother writing for the right one. Accidents happen. Did he send for it or did you?"

"He did. I got mine from my mother. She had a copy at home."

"Did Val open his?"

"Yes. I never open his mail unless it's addressed to both of us."

"I'm going to talk to Jack tonight. He can find someone in the Trumbull police station to check a phone book. It's probably the phone book for the whole area, and we'll see how many Krasskys they come up with. I'll also ask if he can find out the name of the local hospital. This may be worth a trip, Carlotta, but let's not go too soon. Let's see what Jack can dig up for us."

Carlotta got up and walked to the bookcase across the room, leaving behind the questions I had prepared, most of which she had not had the opportunity to ask. Personally, I thought she had done very well. He hadn't hung up on her, which was my greatest fear. He had told us where the child died, and we knew now the boy hadn't been burned beyond recognition or hit by a car or drowned. I stopped my thoughts on the last word. That would have been some coincidence, to be drowned twice. But it hadn't happened.

"All I wanted was to find my husband alive," Carlotta said. "Now I find he died twenty-five years before I met him."

"We'll find out," I said. "The fact that there are strange things going on tells us to keep looking. I have no intention of giving up."

10

"Hey, good to hear your voice, Chris," Jack said in my ear.

"Same here. You just get home?"

"Just walked in. Haven't even looked at the mail yet. How're you feeling?"

"Great."

"Drinking your milk?"

"Carlotta got a gallon of skim, and I'm making my way through it."

"Sounds awful."

"It is. I have things to tell you."

"Let me pull up a chair."

I went through it all, from the insurance policy to the Krasskys in Connecticut, dictating names and addresses, and spelling out my requests. Nothing I asked was impossible, but nothing was certain. Still, when I said good night, I had the feeling I would know a lot more by this time tomorrow.

When I got up in the morning, my first thought was that I was glad I didn't have to catch a plane. I felt awful. I regretted immediately the delicious lobster I had devoured the night before. Flu, I thought miserably. Four hundred miles from home and I have to get sick.

I sat up and became aware that I didn't feel feverish. I pulled on my robe and went to my private bathroom where I looked at myself in the mirror. It wasn't the most pleasing sight I'd ever seen. I washed and brushed my teeth, then brushed my hair, all the while hoping my stomach would calm down.

I went downstairs and found Carlotta putting breakfast together. "I'm afraid I'm not feeling well," I said, pulling a chair out from the breakfast table. "I think the lobster didn't sit well."

"Maybe it's morning sickness," she said.

"Morning sickness." I felt a sense of relief and, I must admit, a bit of pride. "Morning sickness." I was pregnant. This is what happened to other women, and it was happening to me. "I bet that's it. I'm sure I'm not running a temperature."

"What's the antidote? Do you take pills?"

"No, not unless it gets severe. She said dry toast or crackers or something like that. I wish I could drink some tea. It's so soothing."

Carlotta brought a box of long, narrow, crisp toasts to the table, and I broke one and started to eat it. On the stove, a handsome tea kettle was already over a flame.

"I feel like an idiot," I said. "I insulted that lobster wrongfully."

She laughed. "You're forgiven. Is this the first time you've had it?"

"The absolute first. I really thought I was ill. I think I'm feeling better already. Just knowing what it is is a help."

"I've got some English Breakfast. How does that sound?"

"I guess I'd better not. Dr. Campbell frowns on caffeine in any form. I'll just pour myself a glass of milk. As long as I know I'm not dying, I think I'll feel better on my feet."

She looked approvingly at me. "How are the crackers?"

"Very tasty." I stood and munched another, feeling a little giddy. A new experience in my life. I was on my way to being a mother.

"Jake said to drop in anytime," Carlotta said, as we finished our breakfast.

I was feeling much better, the crackers and milk having done their work. "Then I'll dress and drive over."

"When will you hear from Jack?"

"It's hard to say. If he has time, he'll probably call as soon as he has something. If you're here, I'm sure he'll tell you whatever he knows."

"I'll be here. You and Jake don't need me."

I went upstairs, dressed, and made the bed.

Val's daily drive to work was a scant twenty minutes. It struck me as a nice way to live. Jack drives a very long distance now that we're married. His old drive or subway ride from one part of Brooklyn to another has been replaced by a trip from our Westchester suburb southwest into the big city. But here was a man who could get up in the morning, have a leisurely breakfast, and be at work by eight-thirty without trying very hard.

The building that Val's and Jake's business was in was a small, square, three-story construction of red brick. The directory inside the front door showed only one other business on the first floor. Whatever the other offices held, there couldn't have been many employees. Except for mine, there were no cars at the curb, and the small lot behind the building was mostly empty.

When I knocked at the inside door, standing at a glass window so I could be seen, the man inside looked my way and buzzed me in.

"Ms. Bennett?"

"Yes. I'm Chris."

"Jake Halpern." He held out his hand. "Glad to meet you." He opened a door, called someone, and said to me, "We can sit in back and talk. Otherwise I'll be interrupted all morning."

A younger man appeared, and we went back to a cluttered office with cartons piled, strange-looking components scattered, and a desk under siege. Jake emptied a chair for me and took the one at his desk.

"Carlotta said you wanted to talk about Val."

"She thinks he's alive."

"Carlotta would think Val was alive if they found his body in the lake. She can't face the truth. I'm having a damn hard time facing it myself."

"But she has reasons. She thinks he wasn't the kind of man who would do something so stupid."

"I'd like to think she's right. It doesn't look that way."

"Did you know Val's two friends, Matty and Clark?"

"Sure. They'd drop in sometimes. I went out with them once in awhile."

"The impression I get is that Matty exerted a lot of pressure on Clark. If Matty dared Clark to do something, he'd do it."

"That's pretty accurate. Matty was that kind of guy. Clark was more malleable."

"And Val?"

"Different from both, more of his own man. He didn't have an ego like Matty's, and nobody except Carlotta could twist him around their finger. We were in business for a long time together. We got along and we were good friends. I've seen him under fire. He was a guy who could hold his own."

"Then you're saying what Carlotta says: Matty couldn't embarrass him into doing something stupid."

"Right. But he might've done it because he wanted to, because these two guys were his friends, they were in a good mood, crossing the lake to Canada was a challenge, and he was always up for a challenge. There're a lot of reasons why he might have gone with them."

"And you think he did."

"Is there any indication that he didn't?"

I decided not to get into that. "Carlotta and I have done some digging in the last two days, and we've found some interesting things about Val. You knew him for a long time, didn't you?"

"Fifteen years, anyway."

"Did you go to college together?"

"We met there."

"What do you know about his family?"

He smiled for the first time since we had sat down. "OK, you hit the one crazy part of Val's life. I admit it. There was something damn weird about his family."

"Like what?"

"Like whether they existed."

"You mean his parents?"

"Like I'm not sure he even had parents. If he did, he never talked about them. I come from a family that's very close and very outgoing. My father does his thing, my mother does hers, my grandmother would drop in during the day when I was a kid. I have a sister and a brother, and we never stood still, always doing something, always going somewhere. I would say to Val, 'You should see this girl my brother brought home over Christmas. Wow!' or 'My sister's playing the lead in the high school play, and I'm going home to see it.' And we would talk about my family. But in all the years I knew that man, I never once heard him say the words 'my mom' or 'my dad.' If he had brothers and sisters, it's news to me. He would leave college for vacation and drop into a void."

"You mean you don't know where he went?"

"I mean I don't know what planet he went to."

"Did he ever talk about Connecticut?"

"Not that I remember. Hey, can I get you some coffee?"

I was feeling pretty good and I would have loved a cup, but I thought I'd better not. "No thanks," I said. "How did the two of you happen to open your business here?"

"OK, that's a link. He knew western New York. He was the first person I ever met who told me about the Erie Canal. I'm from New York, and the only canal I'd ever heard of was Canal Street in downtown Manhattan. I kicked around a little after school and he did, too. When we got together to think about making our fortune, Val suggested the Buffalo area."

"So he had a connection here."

"Yeah, but don't ask me what it was. Maybe it was Matty and Clark."

"They were here when you opened up?"

"Oh, yeah. I met them right away."

"Do you know their wives?"

"A little."

"Jake, we found Val's birth certificate in the safe deposit box in the bank. He was born in Connecticut."

"If you tell me, I believe it. Maybe he left as a kid, and his memories were just of this area."

"That must be it," I said. "Did you ever meet any of his old girlfriends?"

"Dozens. Val went out a lot. When we first opened up, we shared a flat in a two-family house in Buffalo and commuted out here. Then about a year later, I got married and my wife and I got ourselves a place nearby. Val didn't get married for a few years, and I used to meet his girlfriends when he took them out. Susie and I would go out with them once in awhile or meet them for a drink. Val always dated nice girls, pretty, smart. Once, I remember, he went out with a doctor."

"So there was nothing out of the ordinary there."

"Nothing I saw."

"Were you at his wedding?"

"Sure. We flew out to Ohio."

"Who was there?"

"Her family. That's all."

"And his friends?"

"Goes without saying. Matty and Clark were there with their wives. And some other people Val knew. But I don't think there were any of his sisters or his cousins or his aunts," he said, paraphrasing Gilbert and Sullivan.

"Carlotta told me that Val said his parents had returned to Europe, and he wasn't in contact with them."

"That's new to me. Europe?"

"Germany. East Germany is the impression I got."

"Interesting. Sounds a little wacky."

"I know. And it doesn't ring a bell with you?"

"Never heard it before in my life. Frankly, I figured he was orphaned or came from a split family and didn't get along with either side. But that was his business. I never asked."

"Does he have an office here?"

"Sure." He got up and went to the door. "It's across the hall."

I followed him to a room exactly the size of his, but as different as a room could be. It was tidy, and you could see across it without moving boxes.

"Val's neat," Jake said superfluously. "And he pre-ferred to do a lot of paperwork at home. I can't stand working at home. It gets done here or it doesn't get done."

"Would you mind if I looked through Val's desk?" I asked.

He looked troubled. "I don't know."

"I thought Carlotta said—"

"I know what Carlotta said. Carlotta's not my partner. Legally, Val's alive and missing."

"Have the police been through his things?"

"They came over last week, when his body didn't surface."

"Did they take anything with them?" The Rolodex was on the desk.

"I don't think so. This is all business stuff. OK, go ahead and look around. But don't take anything."

"I won't. I promise."

He walked out, leaving the door ajar. The office was windowless, one good reason, I thought, for Val prefer-ring to work at home. I started with the Rolodex. It was a large one and had hundreds of filled-in cards. I read them quickly, learning nothing except that Val had a lot of contacts, all of which seemed to be businesses. Even the ones that began with a person's name had a business name underneath. I gave up after awhile and looked under *D* for Dad and *M* for Mom, to no avail. But I did find Matty under *F* for Franklin and Clark under *T* for Thayer. Under *K* for Krassky there was nothing.

I went through the desk drawers and found only what looked like business-related papers. There was no gun permit, no old passport, no personal letters, no indication that Val was other than the co-owner of the computer business his wife had described to me.

I went out to the large front area where Jake was talking to a customer whose computer needed repair. Jake filled out a slip, tore off a copy, and they shook hands. When the customer had gone out, I said, "I didn't ask you in so many words, but I don't suppose you've heard from Val since February fourteenth."

"Me? Heard from him?"

"He hasn't called?"

"No, ma'am."

"He didn't show up on the morning of the fifteenth and then disappear?"

"Chris, I saw him on Valentine's Day. He came in in the morning and left before noon. He was wearing a suit and had a small, gift-wrapped package with him."

"Do you know what it was?"

"It was a gift for Carlotta. I never saw it."

"Did he pick it up himself?"

"He picked it out, but I think he said it had to be sized, and he had it delivered here so she wouldn't know about it."

"When did he leave for lunch?"

"Maybe eleven-thirty."

"Did he come back afterwards?"

"He was going to, but he didn't. He had to take Carlotta to the airport in Buffalo. She had a business trip to make. He called in the afternoon and said he wouldn't bother coming in, he could work at home."

"Jake, did Val ever talk to you about making a will?"

"We never talked about things like that."

"So you don't know if he had one or not."

"No idea. My wife and I just had ours done last year when we went away and left our kids behind for the first time. We never felt we needed one before that."

"You have a business that must make a good living for two people. Didn't you think it was necessary to spell out who gets what in case of your death?"

"That's part of our partnership agreement."

"I see. Would you mind telling me what happens to Val's share if he dies?"

"It's a little complicated, but I have the right to buy out his half. We're equal partners. Essentially the value of his half passes to Carlotta, as mine does to Susie, but neither of the wives has any interest or knowledge in the business. We assumed they would want to sell and cash in on the investment. It requires an audit to see what the business is worth. Because of what's happened, both Carlotta and I are in limbo. I can't buy his half because legally he isn't dead."

"Your interests would be best served if he turned up dead."

"I don't like the way that sounds. It's in Carlotta's best interests, maybe. My best interests would be served if Val walked in that door and started to work again."

"What are you doing in his absence?" I asked.

"It ain't easy," he said with a smile. "I've hired

someone to help out because I can't be here alone, but everything the business earns is divided into his half and my half."

"So if he's not declared dead for many years, you're working for two people."

"That's about the size of it. And if Carlotta needs the money Val's half would bring, she can't have it."

"You don't think you could work out some agreement with her?"

"Sure I could. Then Val comes waltzing in with a girl-friend he's been shacking up with, and he doesn't have his income any more. The wife who wasn't supposed to get it has it."

He was right that it was a mess. Val's disappearance didn't help either of them. "Where were you the night of February fourteenth, if you don't mind my asking?"

"At home with my family. Susie picked up a cute heart-shaped cake and we had a little party. I sent her flowers. I have to admit, it's something I learned from Val. In the family I come from, if it wasn't a birthday, it didn't get any attention."

"And when did you find out Val was missing?"

"The next day. He didn't come in at his usual time, but there were no appointments so I didn't think about it."

"Was he usually on time?"

"Always. But the day before was his birthday, and I knew he'd gone out with the guys. If he was a little late, I could live with it."

"How did you find out about the accident?" I persisted.

"Eventually, Carlotta called."

"You never called Val at home?"

"I figured he was sleeping off a late night. I didn't want to wake him."

"So the last time you saw him was walking out the door to meet his wife for lunch."

"That was it."

"And that night he disappeared."

"Look, Chris," he said, "Val didn't disappear. He left his watch in the back of Matty's four-by-four and walked across the lake to Canada. We both know where he is. His body's at the bottom of Lake Erie."

I couldn't argue anymore. I was out of ammunition.

11

I went outside, walked down the path to the car, and started driving back toward the house, thinking about what Jake had said. His partner was always on time, and the one time he was very late, Jake hadn't called to find out if anything was wrong. It didn't sit well somehow. But the truth was, it wasn't to Jake's advantage to have Val missing. If he knew that Val was dead, he would be better off. But how could he know? How could anyone know unless there was a body buried somewhere on dry land? And if the watch was in Matty's locked car, Val had to be at the bottom of the lake.

I was almost back to the house when something occurred to me, and I turned and found my way to the police station. Luckily for me, the desk sergeant said Detective Murdock was in, and he picked up a phone and called him.

"Ms. Bennett," the big man's deep voice boomed as he turned the corner and saw me. "What's up?"

"I have a question."

"Want to sit in the office?"

"No thanks. It's just a quick one. Did you tell me Matty Franklin's car was locked?"

"It sure was. We had to get Mrs. Franklin's key to open it up."

"Those four-wheel drive things, they have a hatchback, don't they?"

"Yeah."

"Was that locked, too?"

He looked at me as though I had said something startling. "I can't say for sure," he said finally. "I wasn't there when they found the vehicle. Why do you ask?"

"Where did they find the watch?"

"In the backseat."

"Was it in plain sight?"

"I don't think it was hidden in any way."

"Suppose Val was killed or grabbed on the beach and the killer opened the hatchback, crawled in, and tossed or dropped his watch on the backseat to make it look like he went across the lake with the others."

"Where's his body?"

"I don't know yet."

"Who knew the men were going to the beach?"

"Someone who followed them from Giordano's."

"OK. It's thin, but I'll grant you it's possible. But I need a body. Do you have a minute?" He seemed perturbed.

"Sure."

"Come to my office."

We went down the hall, and when we got to his office, he dispensed with formalities and went right to his desk, pressing the speakerphone key and dialing while I stood and waited.

"Detective Crannock, how can I help you?" a voice answered.

"This is Al Murdock from the sheriff's office. About

the lake accident, you have the file on the utility vehicle they found on the beach?"

"Right next to me. What do you want to know?"

"Was the hatchback locked, too?"

"Hold on." There were sounds of papers rustling. "Here it is. All four doors locked."

"It's the fifth one I'm interested in, the hatchback. Was that door locked, too?"

"I don't think they checked it at the scene, Al."

"Well somebody must've checked it." Murdock sounded angry. "Who took custody of the car?"

"Take it easy. Lemme look at the officer's inventory sheet. What're you so shook-up about?"

"Sloppy police work, that's what. The guy who found the vehicle, didn't he check the hatchback to see if it was open?"

"Doesn't look like it. Here's the sheet I'm looking for. By the time the car was inventoried, the doors were all open. Can I get back to you? I want to make a call."

"I'm waiting." Murdock hung up and turned to me. "Nothing bothers me more than sloppy police work."

"It probably didn't occur to the poor fellow who found the car that there was another way in or out," I said, trying to explain the officer's oversight.

"Poor fellow," Murdock echoed derisively. Then the phone rang. "Murdock."

"Al, I just talked to the guy who vouchered the vehicle. He says all five doors were unlocked, including the hatchback, when he got it. If you wanted me to take a guess, I'd say it was open the whole time, but I'll follow up on this."

"I wish you would."

"You got something going?"

"I don't know. It's just a nagging question, and I hate nagging questions."

"Almost as much as sloppy police work, right?"

"Right on the button." Murdock disconnected. "I'll let you know anything I hear, Ms. Bennett."

"Thank you."

"But even if your scenario is right, I need a body."

"I'll do my best," I said.

"But who would do it?" Carlotta said, after I explained my conversation with the detective. "It can't be Clark or Matty."

"That's the one thing I'm sure of. We need a motive, Carlotta. Let's talk about Jake."

"You think *Jake* killed Val?"

"I don't know who killed Val. I don't know if Val is dead. I'm just looking for anything that might give me a lead."

"It isn't Jake."

"You seemed very reluctant for me to talk to him. Is there a reason?"

"I wasn't reluctant," she said with a frown. "Maybe I was a little uncomfortable. Jake and Val work so closely together. I don't know."

"Do you like him?"

"Very much."

"And Susie?"

"I adore Susie. We've become friends."

"More than your relationship with Bambi and Annie?"

"Much more. Susie's a very interesting woman. I enjoy talking to her." She stopped for a moment. "Chris, while you were out I called the lawyer who drew up the partnership agreement between Val and Jake. You were right. Val did have a will, and this lawyer drew it up."

"What's in it?" I asked.

"He won't tell me. He said that I am, indeed, a beneficiary—that's how he put it—which doesn't surprise me; I'm the wife. But he says that until Val is officially declared dead, he can't disclose the terms."

"OK. I gather Jack didn't call?"

"No one called."

"Then let's wait and see what Jack has to say. I think the next step is Connecticut."

"Let's have lunch. This is driving me crazy."

I was starting to get the feeling that Carlotta's beautiful kitchen was used only for breakfast, but I didn't mind going out. We went to a new place this time, a small Chinese restaurant that was a longer drive than the nearby tearoom, and we ate a good lunch. When we got back to the house, there were two messages on her machine, one from Detective Murdock and one from Jack. I called Murdock first.

"Ms. Bennett, got a piece of news for you," he said. "I talked to the officer who found the Franklin vehicle on the beach on February fifteenth. He's sure he never tried the hatchback."

"So it could have been open all night."

"And probably was. When the sheriff's people got to the scene, one of the deputies tried it and it was open."

I had the call on the speakerphone, and I could see Carlotta's eyes widen. "Thank you, Detective."

"Thank *you*, Ms. Bennett. You really picked up a flaw in our procedure."

"Let's see where it leads us. That's the important thing."

Carlotta was standing beside the desk when I hung up. "Tell me again. You think someone could have taken Val's watch off his wrist and tossed it into Matty's car."

"That would be why it's in the backseat, because whoever did it had to crawl through the hatchback, which isn't very comfortable. Whoever it was didn't want to make the effort to crawl over the backseat and into the front seat to open the glove compartment. He just leaned over the backseat and dropped it there."

"And you think that means that someone killed Val and hid his body."

"It's possible. That's all I'm saying. Let me call Jack and see what he's come up with."

Carlotta dropped into a chair while I dialed, keeping the call off the speakerphone. I still felt that a conversation with my husband deserved a certain amount of privacy. When I said, "Hello," the same thing seemed to occur to her, too, and she left the room.

"How's it going?" Jack said.

"I had morning sickness this morning," I said, starting with the most important thing first.

"And I missed it. Was it bad?"

"Not really. Carlotta gave me some crackers and I felt better. I thought I had the flu."

"Well I'm glad you didn't. Got some stuff for you. There's another Krassky, an Ivan, in the same phone book as Gregory."

"Sounds like a relative. Got an address?"

He dictated and I wrote. "And I've got the names of some hospitals in the area." He gave them to me, too.

We talked awhile, and I told him about Jake Halpern and about my discovery of the unlocked hatchback.

"Sloppy," he commented, and I smiled.

"I think I'll fly home tomorrow and drive to Connecticut," I said.

"Right from the airport?"

"If I can get a plane that gives me time to get there by afternoon."

"You know, if you're not feeling well in the morning—"

"I hadn't thought of that. OK, I'll let you know what I decide, but I think there isn't much more I can do here. I've talked to the wives and the detective and the partner. Maybe I'll see you tomorrow night for dinner."

"That would be nice. Remind me I have a wife again."

"I miss you."

"But you're busy."

"Very busy."

"Don't forget to call."

I talked it over with Carlotta. She wanted to accompany me to Connecticut, but I asked her not to. I didn't think there was much she could add to a discussion with Ivan Krassky, whoever he was—assuming he agreed to speak to me. She got on the phone and booked me on a flight the next morning to La Guardia. Where Jack and I live, on the north shore of the Long Island Sound, we're on the way to Connecticut, and I thought maybe I'd stop and pick him up and we could enjoy a little time together if he weren't locked into studying his law books. Then I sat down with Carlotta and asked her a lot of questions that had been troubling me.

"Do you know where Val went to high school?"

"In Buffalo," she said. "Bennett High School, I think—like your name. It's a big red brick building on Main Street. We've driven by it." That confirmed what Bambi had told me.

"Did Matty and Clark go there, too?"

"I think so, but I wouldn't swear to it."

"Do you know where Val lived in Buffalo?"

"I don't think he ever mentioned it."

"Jake said Val never talked about his family, that in college when he went home, he'd kind of fall off the face of the earth. Did you ever hear him talk about a family of any sort, his parents or the people he lived with after his parents went back to Europe?"

"He never talked about his parents, and he never talked about any other family. I assumed he lived with his parents. Most kids do."

"Did he ever tell you when his parents left the U.S.?"

"Chris, I really hate these questions. I don't think Val had anything to hide. I don't think where he lived in high school or who he lived with or when his parents went back to Germany have any connection to what happened on Valentine's Day."

"I think they may," I said.

"Why?"

"Because people don't hatch full grown from eggs. Their history is part of them, and often this history gives us an inside picture of why certain things happen to them. Jack says everything connects to something."

"Are you saying that you think Val did something once that made him deserve to be killed?"

"No. I'm saying there are strange things about his background, things that are hard to explain. His relationship to his parents is one of them. He wrote a will and never told you about it and didn't leave a copy in his safe deposit box. That's another. His birth certificate and what we've learned about the Krasskys of Connecticut is certainly weird. Most people have some family somewhere. He has none."

"My father said something about that when I first brought Val home."

"So I'm not the first person to ask these questions."

"I asked some of them, too, Chris," Carlotta said. "Eventually, it didn't matter what the answers were. I loved him. He was the best thing that ever happened to me. Maybe his parents came to this country, had him, got into some trouble with the law, and left to save themselves. I didn't marry Val's mother and father; I married him. He's honorable and good, and I don't give a damn what his family is like."

"I think Jake feels the same way about him. He said the best thing that could happen to him would be to have Val walk in the door and start to work again."

"Jake's a good person." She seemed very down. "I'm scared, Chris. I'm really scared. You're going to find something out in Connecticut that I don't want to know. Maybe the real reason I want to go there with you is to prevent whatever it is from coming out."

"Let's face it when it happens, if it happens. I have some other questions. Bambi said Clark's parents are dead. Did they die while you knew Clark?"

"No. Clark would have told Val. It must have happened years ago."

"What about Matty?"

"What about him?"

"Did he have parents?"

"I assume so."

"Did you see them at the funeral?"

"I don't know. There were older people sitting with Annie. I couldn't tell you who they were."

"Do you mind if I call her?"

"Go ahead." She looked bewildered, as though she had lost her way and didn't know where the path would lead.

I went to Val's study and made the call. Annie answered right away.

"Annie, this is Chris Bennett. I wanted to ask you about Matty's family."

"What family?"

"His parents, his brothers and sisters."

"He was an only child."

"Are his parents alive?"

"His father's dead. His mother lives in England."

"Was Matty born here?"

"Oh, yes. But his parents split up or something a long time ago, before I met him. His mother was from England originally, and she went back."

"Did he keep in touch with her?"

"No, he didn't," Annie said. "He told me he had sided with his father during the divorce, and she refused to have anything to do with him. It's too bad. She's missed having grandchildren."

"It is too bad," I said, thinking, as I always did, that my mother would have loved to know her own grandchild, but she died over fifteen years ago. "Thanks, Annie."

"You find anything yet?"

"Nothing very interesting," I said, minimizing what I now knew.

"There probably isn't anything to find. If Val's body ever turns up, that'll be the end."

I agreed with what she said and ended the conversation.

12

I mulled everything over on the short flight to La Guardia the next day. Nothing seemed to lead anywhere, and every small piece of information I had uncovered had spawned a slew of unanswered questions. This is no way to go, Kix, I said to myself, using the nickname I had grown up with, the gift of my cousin Gene, who had been unable to say "Chris" at an early age.

I had even less hope now of finding Val alive, but I wanted to know who had killed whom and, if possible, why. Murdock had branded Val as Matty's killer, and that unproven charge would stick if nothing else came to light. It might be true—it was very likely to be true—but I wanted to be convinced. And why, I kept asking myself, does a man take out an insurance policy on his life and then murder the beneficiary? Why not just cancel the policy or change the beneficiary?

Outside my window I could see the endless miles of New York's buildings. I had never unfastened my seat belt, but the sign had just gone on, and I could hear the clicks of other passengers' as they readied themselves for our descent and landing. It was a clear day, and the city looked almost sparkling. In a little while, I would be down where the sparkle was less evident, but for a few minutes I enjoyed the view.

Jack was waiting for me as I turned up the driveway. We had decided over the phone last night that I would stop and pick him up and we would drive to Connecticut together. He came outside and we hugged and kissed and did it all over again. Then he grabbed my suitcase, and we went inside together.

In the living room, I took my coat off and Jack gently patted my abdomen.

"Still pretty flat," he said.

"With all I've been eating, it should be puffing out."

"How was this morning?"

"About the same as yesterday. Carlotta actually brought me breakfast in bed. I couldn't believe it. I've never been treated so luxuriously."

"Not even by your husband. I see this case is going to change my life."

"Not as much as this baby. Any word when they're breaking ground for the addition?"

"It's still any day. You thinking of staying away till they finish?"

"If you can live through it, I can. You ready for Connecticut?"

"Yup. I've got maps, addresses, routes, everything you need."

"Great. Let me take a look at the mail, and then let's go."

I poured out everything I knew as Jack drove to Connecticut. He asked a number of questions, and they were pretty much the ones I had no answers for. Somehow those Krasskys in Connecticut had to have the key to all this.

"I have to say," Jack said, "that insurance policy is really intriguing. Did you tell Murdock about it?"

"No. There's a lot I didn't tell Murdock, including the birth certificate. He thinks his missing man is a killer. I don't want to add any fuel to his hot theory."

"What's different about this is that there was no suspicion a crime had been committed till more than two months after it happened. So if there was something to find on land, it's become obscured."

"Melted away," I said.

"Right. Like the footprints in the snow on the lake. You know, I think we're almost there."

I took another look at one of the maps, and then at the street sign we were just passing. "You're right. Ivan Krassky's house should be about two blocks from here. It looks like a right."

"Nice area."

"Beautiful. Look at those trees."

Jack made the turn and drove slowly down a street lined with brick and stone houses shaded with old, large trees. "Should be a couple of houses down. Why don't I park here and you can walk? It's better if they don't see me. I've been told I'm very threatening."

I laughed out loud. "You? Threatening? If you'd been threatening, I'd still be single."

"Watch what you say, lady. My whole career may go up in smoke."

I leaned over and kissed him. Then I got out of the car and walked down the street.

The woman who opened the door was in her sixties or late fifties—I'm terrible at judging age—dressed in a denim skirt and a man-tailored shirt. She was pleasantly rounded, and her expression verged on a smile. "Yes?" she asked.

"Mrs. Krassky?"

"That's me."

"My name is Christine Bennett. I'm here because a man named Krassky was apparently killed in an accident a couple of months ago in western New York State."

"A Krassky?"

"Yes. His first name was Valentine." I watched her face change.

She shook her head. "That's an odd coincidence."

I handed her a copy of the newspaper article from the Buffalo paper. She read it, taking in a breath at the point where I assumed she was reading Val's name and age. Finally she looked up. "Who did you say you were?"

I showed her my driver's license, the only ID I carry with my picture on it. "I'm a friend of Val Krassky's wife."

"Come inside."

I went into her living room and stood while she finished reading the article. "This must be a coincidence," she said.

"His birth certificate is from Connecticut."

"Just a minute. Let me get my husband." She left the room, and I heard her call, "Ivan? Can you come inside for a minute?" Then the two of them walked into the living room. "Ivan, this lady—I'm sorry, what did you say your name was?"

"Chris Bennett."

"Yes. She says a man named Valentine Krassky was killed in an accident in—" she searched the article "—in February. Good heavens. Did it happen on Valentine's Day?"

"It did."

"I'm Ivan Krassky," the man said, offering me his hand. He was well into his sixties, I estimated, with a rather nice salt-and-pepper beard and hair to match. "Can you tell me what this is about?"

"I know there's another Krassky in the area who had a child named Valentine about thirty-five years ago," I said.

"That's my brother."

"And I've been told Valentine died as a child."

"He did," the wife said. "It was a terrible tragedy."

"I thought perhaps you might have had a son with the same name," I said, feeling a little silly.

"We have sons, but none with that name," Ivan said.

"This accident on Lake Erie took the lives of three men, one of them named Valentine Krassky. His birth certificate says that his father's name is Gregory, and it gives a Trumbull address and a local hospital."

"It sounds like he's an imposter."

"Tell me how the child died," I said, as we all sat.

"It was one of those childhood illnesses that took a turn for the worse," Mrs. Krassky said. "He was only six or seven years old, poor little thing, and he couldn't breathe. I think he actually died of pneumonia."

"My brother and his wife never got over it."

"I can understand that. Please bear with me. I'm trying to find an explanation for what looks like a strange coincidence, your nephew who died at the age of six or seven and a man exactly the same age with the same name who lived almost thirty years longer. Are you absolutely certain that child died?"

Husband and wife looked at each other. Then Ivan said, "As sure as I can be without having seen the body. We went to the funeral."

"Greg and his wife donated little Val's organs, the ones that weren't harmed by the pneumonia," Mrs. Krassky said. "They told us about it later. They got a call from the hospital, it must have been early morning, and were told Val had died. And then they were asked almost immediately if they would donate some of his organs. You can imagine how they felt, the shock of learning their son was dead and having to make that terrible decision, all at once. I don't know how they survived it."

"Then they weren't with him when he died?"

"They'd gone home for the night. After they brought him in, he seemed to be improving. The doctor said there was nothing to worry about. Then they got the call."

"Do you know if they actually saw their son's body after he died?"

They looked at each other. "I don't think it was ever mentioned," she said. "It's not the sort of thing you ask."

"Are you trying to say Val didn't die?" Ivan asked.

"I'm just trying to understand what happened. A thirty-five-year-old man apparently died in a lake accident near Buffalo on Valentine's Day. His wife knew him as Valentine Krassky. In his safe deposit box was the birth certificate for your nephew. Val obtained it when he applied for a passport a couple of years ago. From what we've been able to find out, Val's early life is a little cloudy. He told his wife his parents were from East Germany and had to return there. According to her, he had no contact with them. No letters came from Germany, no phone calls were made there in the last year. I checked the phone bills myself."

"There has to be a simple answer for this," Ivan said. He was clearly perturbed. He got up, tugged at his beard, walked around the living room. "A child died and is reincarnated in another place? I don't buy it."

"I don't buy that either," I assured him. "I'm looking for a reasonable explanation."

"Ivan," his wife said, "wasn't there some funny business in the hospital when Val died?"

Ivan stopped and thought for a moment. "There was. It's so long ago, I'd almost forgotten. Greg threatened to sue."

"They made a settlement," she said. "It never got to court."

"What did they want to sue about?" I asked.

"Some kind of malpractice or malfeasance. They left a child who was improving, and they buried a child who died a few hours later. My sister-in-law probably blames herself to this day that she didn't stay overnight in Val's room."

"But they actually settled? The hospital paid your brother and his wife to keep it out of court?"

"Absolutely," Ivan said. "You know," he turned to his wife, "I haven't thought about that for a long time. Sure they got paid."

"And they moved," his wife said. "Irene said she couldn't bear to live in that house with Val's room as if he might come back at any time. I have no idea how much they got, but I'm sure they used some of it to buy the new house."

"Maybe my next stop should be the hospital," I said.

"I doubt they'll tell you anything," Ivan said. "They've probably got those records sealed up so tight they can't find them themselves."

"Maybe someone there will remember." I stood. "Could you give me the name of the hospital?" I passed him my notebook and a pen. "Was the little boy buried in a cemetery around here?"

"Gate of Heaven," Mrs. Krassky said. "It's not far."

I added that in my notebook when Ivan handed it back to me. He had scribbled some driving instructions to the hospital, and I thanked him.

"I hope you'll let us know what happens. This is very intriguing. You've got me wondering about that whole sad episode all over again. If someone in that hospital grabbed that little boy, called Greg, and said he'd died and they needed to take his organs to give to some deserving kid, who would know, if they never saw Val dead?"

"Nothing fits yet, Mrs. Krassky. When—if—I put it together, I'll let you know." I wrote down my name, address, and phone number and gave it to them. "Thank you for your help."

They walked me to the door, and I went down the block to where Jack was standing unthreateningly outside the car, taking in the fresh air and sunshine.

I briefed him on my conversation with the Krasskys as we drove to the hospital.

"Their business office may not be open today," Jack said. "It's Saturday, in case you've forgotten. You folks who work every day of the week sometimes forget that weekend schedules are different."

"I know. But just on the chance that someone's there, let's try. I can always come back on Monday."

"Anyway, it's a nice day for a drive."

The front desk directed me to a small office where one woman sat at a desk covered with papers. I did my best but it was a fruitless mission. She said she didn't have access to old records on the weekend, that a thirty-year-old case was pre-computer, and the paper files would be locked up in the basement, inaccessible until Monday. When she was all finished telling me why she couldn't possibly help me, she added that probably no one else would help me either, on Monday or any other day, since medical records were private and I was not considered an interested party. Then she smiled and said she had a lot of work to do and would I excuse her.

I found Jack wandering around the ground floor. "Hopeless," I said more cheerfully than I felt.

"She can't get them on the weekend in the first place, and you're not entitled to medical records in the second place. Or vice versa."

"Were you eavesdropping?"

"Just telling it like it is, sweetheart. Getting information from a hospital without a shield or a court order does not qualify as easy duty."

"What I need is someone who worked there thirty years ago," I said, thinking out loud, as we walked to the parking lot.

"You are a digger, honey. If I'd hooked up with you ten years ago, I'd be a captain by now."

"You're too young to be a captain."

"Some guys make it young."

"Besides, I like you better as a law student."

"You don't have much choice. So what'll it be—dinner in Connecticut or dinner in New York State?"

"Hmm. The unknown verses the known. Tough decision. We're not in a hurry. Let's take a leisurely drive back and see what throws itself in our path."

"If you say so."

We drove out of the parking lot and turned toward home.

13

We found a restaurant in Connecticut around six o'clock that had just opened for dinner and had a free table, and we had a truly good meal. When we left a couple of hours later, people were driving up in Mercedes and Jaguars, the women wearing glitter in their hair and on their hands, for dinner at a more fashionable hour. For my part, I was happy to have eaten early, even happier to get home at a reasonable hour. I called Greenwillow, the home for retarded adults where my cousin Gene lives, and said I would pick him up the next morning in time for ten o'clock mass. I didn't invite him to Sunday dinner because the cupboard was bare. I had shopping to do, and Jack had the studying he had put off to accompany me to Connecticut.

At home there was a message from the builder that if the weather was good, he would like to get started on our addition on Monday morning. A few days before Carlotta had called with the news that the two bodies had surfaced, the foundation had been dug three feet deep in our backyard and the concrete slab on which the addition would sit had been poured. Now we were ready for the framing.

While we were both very anxious to get it done, it

meant we would have to vacate our present bedroom, onto which the addition would be attached, and that meant moving furniture. The bed could be disassembled and reassembled fairly easily, but the dresser and chest were heavy pieces. Our friend and neighbor Hal Gross had offered to help when the time came, and it looked as if this was it. I suffered a recurring attack of "do-I-really-want-to-do-this-itis," but the concrete slab was there and the next step was upon me. I called the Grosses.

Sunday after mass I ducked out of the house at Jack's request and went down the block to the Grosses', as Hal came in the other direction to help Jack. Mel was alone, her mother having swooped up the grandchildren and disappeared with them.

"So how are you feeling?" Mel asked as we sat in the family room.

"Had my first morning sicknesss the last three days."

"Is it bad?"

"Just enough that I know something's cooking."

"Something's definitely cooking." She smiled her great smile. "Do you think you'll keep teaching after you give birth?"

"I'd like to. It's only one morning a week, and I can do all the rest of the work at home. I need to do something with my mind."

"I know. That's the hardest part of being a mother, especially when they're so little. I've been thinking about going back to teaching next fall. There may be an opening in the little school." "Little school" was the common name of the local K-through-four that all our children would eventually attend. "It's just finding someone I trust that's the problem."

"I know," I said, understanding firsthand for the first

time in my life. "Well, I'm not going to think about it for a while. There's a pregnant teacher who's giving birth after the semester starts. She said she'll finish the fall semester for me. I'll have the final ready for her."

"Good planning," Mel said. "Everything's under control and you'll be covered. Jack said you were out of town. What's new?"

"My favorite question." I leaned forward and told her the whole story.

"You think that poor little child never died?" Mel said when I had finished telling her about yesterday in Connecticut.

"I don't know. Nothing holds water at this point. If Val really remembered where he was born and who his parents were, I have to believe he would have gone back to them."

"At least when he got older."

"Or called them. Six-year-olds know their phone numbers."

"Among other things."

"Carlotta knows what high school her husband went to. We'll have to try to find out where he lived during those years. If the school can dig up the records, I can talk to neighbors. But I have this eerie feeling that no one will remember him. He seems to have been invisible or transparent."

"Until Carlotta met him."

"Or a few years before that, when he went into business with Jake Halpern."

"Didn't you say he had two friends who died with him on the lake?"

"They're weird, too, Mel. The parents of one are dead,

and the other's father is dead and his mother lives in England and he had nothing to do with her."

"This is a crazy story."

"I know."

"You'll figure it out," she said breezily. "You always do."

Just because I "always do" doesn't mean I will this time, I thought as I meandered back down the street to our house after Hal's return home. There seemed to be so many barricades in my way on this one. I had never dealt with a hospital before and had never considered that medical information was private, and rightly so. That meant that trying again tomorrow would be as futile as yesterday's attempt. Well, I had the care and feeding of the Brooks family to think of, and maybe emptying my head of the mysterious life and death of Valentine Krassky would help in the long run.

What I eventually came to think of as the turning point in the case came that evening in the form of a phone call from Ivan Krassky's wife.

"Chris?" she said when I answered. "This is Evelyn Krassky, Ivan's wife. Did the hospital tell you anything yesterday?"

"Nothing at all. The woman in the business office said the records weren't accessible on Saturday, and they were private besides. The message I got was that it was useless for me to come back."

"That's what we thought would happen. We've been talking about nothing but that whole dreadful affair since you left."

"I'm sorry to have stirred it all up again."

"But I think we may be able to help you."

"That would be great," I said.

"We can't go to my in-laws."

"I understand that."

"It's too painful for them to talk about it, and I wouldn't want them to think that we were interested in the money or thought that little Val might be alive. But we have a friend who's a retired surgeon who practiced in that hospital. Ivan called him a little while ago. He said he'll talk to you."

"That's wonderful."

"He'll be playing golf tomorrow morning, but if you can be here at eleven, I'll drive you over to his house."

"Thank you, Evelyn. I'll be there."

I hung up, totally forgetting that builders would appear tomorrow morning to start their work, that they might have questions to ask me, that I might regret not being around. I was all caught up in the great chase.

I'm not quite sure how I got out the door on Monday morning. The builders were as good as their word, arriving before eight while I was out for my daily walk, which Dr. Campbell highly approved of. I had bought some crackers like Carlotta's to stabilize my queasy morning stomach, and having nibbled at one I left the house with a second one. Down the block Mel joined me.

"I'm terrified all over again," I said as we got in step. "It's really happening."

"You talking about the baby or the addition?"

"The addition. It's more imminent and may take a bigger toll on me. My life won't be my own anymore. My bedroom is disappearing, my kitchen won't be the same, and my life is going to be full of strangers."

"And boy, are you going to be happy when it's all done."

"I know."

"Have they given you a date?"

"Yes, but everyone says not to believe it. I'm hoping it's all done by Labor Day."

"That seems like adequate time. Is that their truck?"

I looked up the block and sure enough, there was a maroon truck heading for my house. "That's it," I said. "I should go back."

"Calm down. You've got a competent husband back there who knows how to cope. Finish your walk. It'll help you deal with your day."

I took a quick look back and saw the truck pull into our driveway. Then I did what my friend had suggested. I finished my walk.

I arrived at Evelyn Krassky's house a little before eleven, and she greeted me like an old friend. I had kept a box of crackers on the seat next to me as I drove, and from time to time I would eat half of one. By the time I got there, I was thirsty and the morning discomfort had passed completely.

"The man we're going to meet is Dr. Lyle Windham. He's a real dear and I know you'll love him. Lyle retired several years ago; he's well into his seventies now. He told us he remembers the case of our nephew very well."

"Then he's just the person I want to talk to."

"We can go on along now. He just wanted time to get home from the golf course. Come. We'll take my car."

Dr. Windham's house was almost hidden from the road behind a row of shrubs taller than I. We drove up a private drive that was more like a road to a large stone house that you could have put several of ours in. Evelyn left the car on a circle in front of the double doors, and we got out and rang the bell.

There were effusive hellos and kisses when Mrs. Windham opened the door, then a more discreet shaking of hands when I was introduced.

"Lyle's out back," our hostess said. "Would you ladies mind sitting on the terrace?"

We both said we would prefer that to being inside, and Mrs. Windham led us through several rooms to French doors that opened onto a beautiful brick terrace where the silver-haired doctor sat reading the paper. He rose as we joined him, kissing Evelyn and shaking my hand with a firm grip. He was a tall, handsome man still wearing a green golfing shirt and looking about as fit and trim as a man half his age.

We sat in patio chairs, and Mrs. Windham left us and returned a minute later with iced tea in tall glasses with fresh mint leaves and a platter of the kind of assorted cookies that are my downfall. I could see I was going to do no better at home than I had done in western New York with Carlotta.

"Tell me how you've come to be interested in the death of Evelyn's nephew," the doctor said when we were settled.

I sketched it out for him, the Valentine's Day accident on Lake Erie, the surfacing of the two bodies, the questions about Val's involvement in the murder of Matty and about Val's disappearance. Then I told him about the birth certificate.

"Well, I'll do what I can to help. I wasn't involved in the hospital's financial settlement with Evelyn's in-laws, and everything I know is hearsay, so I feel pretty free about telling you what I know."

"I'm glad to hear it. The hospital itself won't tell me a thing."

"Which is right and proper. Now let me tell you what I know and how I know it."

I had my notebook open and I uncapped my pen. The doctor had bright blue eyes, and he kept them on me as though no one else were present. But Evelyn sat forward in her seat as he began to talk, and Mrs. Windham smiled as though she knew a secret and was way ahead of us.

"I heard about the case because my best friend was a pediatrician at the hospital, and the Krassky boy had been his patient since birth. If my friend were alive, he could tell you chapter and verse—if he were free to—but I'm afraid we lost him a couple of years ago. The child, as I remember the story, had had several bouts with upper respiratory infections and had been brought into the emergency room on a couple of prior occasions, but this incident seemed worse than the others. Chuck—the pediatrician—decided to hospitalize him when the parents brought him in that afternoon. Chuck dashed over from his office to see him, got him going on antibiotics, put him in an oxygen tent—they don't use masks with children—and got him stabilized in a couple of hours. His temperature went down, his breathing improved, he woke up and talked to his parents, who had been pretty panicky when they brought him in. But everyone calmed down, and Chuck told them to go home for the night; there was nothing to be gained by being there. They could come back first thing in the morning. So they left."

"Was there any private care for the child?" I asked.

"There was, a registered nurse who did a lot of private

nursing at the hospital. Don't ask me for her name, because thirty years is a long time. She's the person who discovered the child had died."

"What do you mean, 'discovered'?"

"He wasn't being monitored—remember, this happened almost thirty years ago, and he had improved after being admitted—and when a nurse sits in a hospital room, she doesn't keep her eyes on her patient every minute that she's there. She also leaves the room from time to time to use the bathroom or stretch her legs, and she takes a break for a meal. Eight hours is a long time to sit."

"What happens when she leaves the room for lunch?" I asked.

"Well, that's an interesting thing," Lyle Windham said, his voice becoming more conversational. "When a patient has no private nurse, the floor nurses stop in from time to time to check up on him. But when a private nurse is there, the floor nurses tend to ignore the patient completely. The private nurses know this, and when they leave the room for any period, they let the floor nurses know that they're going down to the cafeteria and can be called if anything comes up."

"Then someone might look in on him once or twice while the private nurse is gone."

"Depending on how long she takes, half an hour or so, maybe less."

"So the story is, she left the room, and when she returned the boy was dead."

"That's about it."

"She didn't see him die."

"She said she wasn't there when it happened."

"Was there anything suspicious about his death?"

"Didn't appear to be. He'd been admitted with pneumonia. That's presumably what he died of."

"Presumably?"

"There were some stories that surfaced later."

"What kind of stories?"

"The kindest version was that the boy received less than adequate care."

"And that means?"

"That something was overlooked, that he should have been in intensive care." The doctor sipped his iced tea and put the glass back on the little round table beside him.

"Do you believe that?"

"Frankly, no. Chuck was as careful a doctor as I have ever met. Still, everyone makes mistakes."

I wondered whether he was talking about himself when he said "everyone." "You said that was the kindest version. Was there another one?"

"Indeed there was. The poor nurse came in for a lot of flak. The family, of course, blamed her for leaving him, which she had a right to do, for not noticing that the boy wasn't breathing easily. She said he was or she wouldn't have left the room."

"Was she known in the hospital?"

"Known and respected. She did duty there almost every night of the week. If I'd needed a private nurse, I would have hired her myself. But, as I said, everyone makes mistakes."

I had the feeling he was trying to tell me something without saying it aloud, but I couldn't proceed on innuendo. "Do you think she told the truth?"

"I think so," he said easily. "I don't think she would have left the room if the boy had become agitated, if his breathing was labored. My best guess is that she would have called a doctor."

"I suppose nurses fall asleep on the job," I suggested.

"I suppose they do. It's pretty boring work when you come down to it, and sitting in the half dark is pretty conducive to sleep."

"Are you suggesting there was a more sinister explanation for the boy's death?"

"There was, and I heard it."

Beside me, Evelyn Krassky drew in her breath. "Lyle, you don't mean to say that someone killed that poor child?"

"Evelyn, I'm just reporting on what I heard. I wasn't there, Chuck wasn't there; rumors circulated and I heard them. That doesn't happen every time a patient dies. It happened that time."

"What was the rumor?" I asked.

"It was said that someone on the floor provoked the child's death."

It was a rather gentle way of saying that the boy had been murdered. A chill ran across my shoulders. "Did the parents get wind of that rumor?"

"My gut tells me they didn't or there would have been much more of a hullaballoo. They blamed Chuck, they blamed the hospital, and they blamed the private nurse. The medical record absolved Chuck, at least that's the way the hospital saw it, and the nurse was adamant that there was nothing wrong with the boy the last time she saw him. My guess is that the hospital paid off because they wanted to stop the parents before they launched a thorough investigation."

"And did it stop them?"

"It must have. The rumors died down or were replaced

by others, perhaps a little spicier, a little more fun to talk about."

"Dr. Windham, was there a particular person who was rumored to have 'provoked' the child's death?" I echoed his euphemism so as not to use the harsher word it implied.

"I believe there was, and I'll come back to that in a minute. Do you have any other questions?"

"I've heard that some organs were donated."

"Well, organ transplants were in their infancy thirty years ago. I think it was only the boy's eyes, which were donated to an eye bank."

"Do you have any idea whether the parents saw the boy's body after he died?"

"I don't know the answer to that. With the eyes removed, they may not have wanted to."

"Do you think there was any way that someone might have switched that boy with a dead child?"

His handsome face clouded. "You mean the nurse found a different child dead in the Krassky boy's bed?"

"Could that have been possible?"

"I don't see how. She'd been with him for several hours. She knew what he looked like."

"My goodness," Mrs. Windham said, "this is certainly taking a morbid turn."

"I'm just trying to consider every possibility," I said. "Was there an autopsy, do you know?"

"My recollection is that the parents didn't want one, and it wasn't required since his death was explainable medically."

"How certain are you that his eyes were actually removed?" I asked.

"Very certain. I'm the surgeon who removed them."

14

That certainly seemed to end the possibility that Val had survived and been kidnapped, although for the life of me I could not imagine what motive anyone would have for "provoking" the death of a six-year-old. "So you know for sure that the eyes were removed, you're pretty sure there was no autopsy, and you don't know whether the parents ever saw the body of their son."

"Right on all three counts."

"Then that leaves the matter you said you would come back to, the person who was suspected—or rumored—to have 'provoked' the death of the child."

"I don't mean to use a pun, but I'm on very thin ice here," the doctor said. "No charges were ever brought, and the police were never called in. There was scuttlebutt and one observable fact."

"Which was?"

"The rumored person left the hospital and never returned."

"I see." I wrote in my notebook, feeling a prickle of excitement. "Will you tell me more?"

"It was a nurse's aide. She'd been there for a while—I can't really tell you how long. After awhile you start to recognize faces. I did most of my work during the day, but I was told she'd been working on that floor for a year, give or take."

"What can you tell me about her?"

"Since I never knew her myself, it's all secondhand. She was probably around thirty, a nurse's aide, no complaints about her that I ever heard. Spoke with an accent."

"One of the Spanish aides?" Evelyn said. "There are so many now from South America."

"This was almost thirty years ago," Dr. Windham said. "She wasn't Spanish as far as I know. More like German is what I heard."

"German," I repeated. "Val told his wife his parents were German and had gone back to Germany."

The doctor's lips formed a small smile. "I leave it to you to make the connections. That's out of my league. All I can tell you is what I know and what I heard."

"Tell me, Doctor, if someone—whoever it was—had murdered that child, how could it have been done?"

"A number of ways," he said easily. "Smother him. Turn off the oxygen and let him suffocate in the tent. He was on an IV; add poison to the drip. If he'd been diagnosed with pneumonia, no one would bother checking the solution. It would be assumed he died of heart failure, one of the consequences of pneumonia."

As he spoke my stomach turned in what was surely not an episode of morning sickness. I felt a fierce protectiveness for the tiny thing inside me that was my child. How could anyone have done to a child any of the things the doctor had just described? "And a nurse or nurse's aide would be aware of those methods?"

"As aware as I am."

"I just can't see a motive," I said, thinking out loud.

"To be honest, I can't either. Maybe Evelyn can enlighten us. Did your in-laws have a dispute with a nurse's aide, or perhaps with the husband of a nurse's aide?"

Evelyn looked completely at sea. "As far as I know they never knew a nurse's aide personally in their lives. If the wife of one of Greg's friends or business associates was a nurse's aide, they never mentioned it. This all seems very surreal. I feel as though we're talking about a science fiction movie."

I felt the same way, but the fact that there was this suspicion concerning the death of the child Val Krassky made a connection with the missing adult Val Krassky somehow more likely. "Do you know how soon after the death of the child the aide left the hospital?"

"Not with any certainty, but fairly soon," the doctor said. "Probably what fueled the speculation that she had something to do with the death."

"Who would know?" I asked.

"It's a long time ago, but I may know someone who can help." He looked over at his wife. "You have that name, dear?"

Mrs. Windham took a slip of paper out of her skirt pocket and passed it to her husband.

"I did a little phoning around after Evelyn called yesterday. This is a very fine lady who was a nurse at the hospital for many years and is long retired. She's in her eighties now, but there's nothing wrong with her memory." He smiled. "It's probably better than mine." He looked at the slip of paper, then passed it to me. "I spoke to her last night. She'll tell you what she remembers."

"I'm very grateful."

"She's about twenty miles from here. I can tell you how to get there."

"I can't thank you enough."

"If you put two and two together and they come out to four, I'd appreciate a phone call."

"I'll see that you get one," I said with the enthusiasm I was suddenly feeling. I had no idea where this new information was going to take me, but I had the strong feeling that for the first time since I had spoken to Carlotta back in February, something was starting to open up.

Evelyn Krassky was utterly enamored of the new developments and was anxious to accompany me to see Mrs. Jane Galotti, but I managed to dissuade her. She was a friend of the Windhams and had served as my introduction to them, but this was a separate lead and I was acting on Carlotta's behalf. I didn't think it was appropriate for her, or anyone else, to be part of my interview. She agreed, and we drove back to her house, where I picked up my car and headed off to Mrs. Galotti's.

Dr. Windham had called before I left his house, and Mrs. Galotti had said this would be a fine time for me to drop by. The twenty miles took half an hour or more, since I kept off highways and drove on scenic roads, passing through several pretty towns with main streets full of charm and low buildings. Mrs. Galotti lived in an old house with a front porch and some beautiful trees shading her front windows. Her lawn was green and the trees were in full leaf, and I thought once again how much I loved this time of year. Added to that, the air had a clean smell, and the fresh foliage added to the scent.

I climbed the several steps to the porch and rang the doorbell. The woman who answered wore her gray hair pulled back in an old-fashioned bun, and her face crinkled into a warm smile when she saw me.

"Miss Bennett?"

"Yes." I offered my hand. "Mrs. Galotti, I'm glad to meet you."

"Come inside. I've got water boiling. I always like a nice cup of tea in the afternoon, and my daughter-in-law dropped off some brownies yesterday. You like brownies?"

"More than I should."

"Well, that's good. It shows a sweet disposition."

More like a sweet tooth, I thought as I went into her kitchen with her, admiring the plants she had arranged in front of the open windows.

"It's still too cold at night to put them out, but I like them to breathe the good outside air. I like to breathe it myself," she said with a laugh. "Make yourself comfortable. The tea'll be ready in a minute. Dr. Windham said you wanted to talk about that little boy who died a long time ago. Isn't the doctor a wonderful man?"

"He seemed very nice. He said you had a terrific memory."

"Well, not as good as you'd like, I think. I can't for the life of me put a name on that nurse's aide, but I can tell you all about her."

"That's good enough. And maybe in a day or two it'll come back to you."

"Could be, could be." I turned down the tea as she went to the stove and took the kettle off, then poured the boiling water into a cup with a tea bag in it and brought it to the table. "We're lucky here, we've got gas. I hate those electric stoves that most people have. This is a good gas stove. Do you do much cooking?"

It was a question that always made me uncomfortable. "Some. I married a man who loves to cook, and he's a lot better at it than I. But I'm learning. A friend taught me how to bake Christmas cookies," I said, mentioning my crowning culinary achievement.

"Well, Christmas cookies will always keep you popular." She set herself carefully in the chair next to mine, as though all the joints from the waist down caused a familiar and dreaded pain. I tried not to wince, feeling for her. Then she squeezed a piece of lemon into her tea and stirred it slowly. "Now, what would you like to know?"

"Dr. Windham said you were a nurse at the hospital he practiced in."

"Forty-seven years. A lifetime career. Loved almost every minute of it."

"Tell me what you know about the death of the little Krassky boy, and tell me how you know it."

"That must have been about thirty years ago. I've been racking my brain since Dr. Windham called last night. Thirty years ago I was fifty-three and in very good shape, if I do say so myself. I was a day nurse on the children's floor, had been for many years. I knew every nurse and every aide who worked days, and I knew the night people because nurses going off duty gave report on the patients and conditions to those coming on. In those days, giving report was very important. Nowadays they run in ten minutes before shift change. It's not the same. I'd get there before eight in the morning, and I worked till four in the afternoon. This woman, whatever her name was, always waited till the morning shift came on before leaving, I'll say that for her. She wasn't one to skip out early. So I got to know her well enough to say, 'Good morning, and how are you today?' "

"Do you know how long she worked at the hospital?"

"Well, she wasn't new when she left. I must have seen her for the best part of a year."

"Can you guess how old she was?"

"A lot younger than me. She must've been thirty, thirty-five, something like that."

"You remember what she looked like?"

"Dark hair. Maybe just a little plump. I shouldn't talk. I got that way myself, even with all the running I did."

"Do you know if she had a family?"

"She wore a wedding ring. I remember that especially because she wore it on her right hand, and I asked her once about it. She told me that was the way they did it in Germany."

"I see. Did she ever mention a husband or children?"

"I'm not sure about that. Could be she did, could be she didn't. We weren't what you would call friends."

"Is there anything you remember about her besides her looks and her wedding ring?"

"Her accent. Her English was pretty good, but she talked with a heavy accent."

"And you think it was a German accent."

"I think so. It wasn't Italian, I'll tell you that." She laughed.

"Now I'd like to know about the little boy, Val Krassky. Were you there when his parents brought him in?"

"Yes," she said firmly. "I was working on the floor that day. I can't tell you exactly what time he came to the hospital, but it had to be before four. I assume they took him to emergency, and then he was admitted and brought upstairs to pediatrics. That's the first I saw him."

"Was his doctor with him?" I asked.

"Dr. Fowler? What a saint that man was. He would do anything for a child, bless his heart. He was there. I saw him with my own eyes."

"And the parents?"

"They came up to the room a little later. Nice people, scared to death, but how could you blame them? Poor little thing was so sick."

"Did you go into his room?"

"Yes, I did, at least once before I went off duty. I talked to the parents, I checked the oxygen tent. Everything seemed to be going very well."

"He was breathing all right?"

"He improved pretty quick, that's what I remember. Once they get that antibiotic in them and that good pure oxygen, it starts to work. His breathing was better, but he looked pale. He was a sick little boy."

"Were the parents there when you went off duty?"

"I'm sure they were. They didn't want to leave, even when Dr. Fowler told them it was safe to go."

"Mrs. Galotti, I hear a lot nowadays about parents spending the night in a child's hospital room. Was that sort of thing done in your hospital?"

"Don't forget, dear, we're talking almost thirty years ago. They do a lot of things today they didn't do then. Now they have special arrangements, rooms with an extra bed for a mother to sleep in. It was a lot more unusual thirty years ago. They could have done it if it had been necessary, but what I heard, Dr. Fowler told them to go home, and if he said so, then it was the right thing.

The boy was doing better, and sitting up all night in a chair doesn't make for a good night."

"So you think they went home because Dr. Fowler told them to."

"I know it," Jane Galotti said.

"How do you know?"

"Everyone said so later. And he called a private nurse for them, and as soon as she got there, the parents left."

"The private nurse, did you know her?"

"Oh, yes. She'd worked in our hospital for years. You get to know them after awhile. She was one of the best. You get to know who's good and who's not so good. Some of them are lazy, some of them sleep all night and the patient has to yell to get them up if they want a glass of water. But she was good, took her work seriously. I would have hired her in a minute myself. Pity you can't talk to her about that night, but she died years ago."

"Did you talk to her after that night?"

"Oh, I talked to her all right, ran into her in the store a couple of days later. She was a wreck. We sat and had a cup of coffee, and she told me the whole thing. Later, she wouldn't say a word to anyone because of the lawyers."

"What did she say?"

"The boy was doing fine. She said she'd gone to the hospital as soon as Dr. Fowler called. She put in extra time that night, got there long before midnight and promised to stay till eight in the morning. The child was sleeping like an angel, breathing nice and regular, everything was fine. Hazel, that's her name," Mrs. Galotti said, pleased to remember it. "Hazel took a lunch break around three in the morning. She let the nurse at the nurses' station know she was going, and she went down to the cafeteria. She hadn't known she'd be working that night or she would have brought her own lunch, but since it was spur-of-the-moment, she had to go down and buy some." She seemed at pains to explain the woman's absence.

"I understand," I said, just to let her know she had my sympathy.

"And then she came back, and the poor little thing was dead."

"Did she see that immediately?"

"Right away. She walked in and started checking up on him. He was just gone."

"What did it look like to her?" I asked.

"Looked like his little heart just gave out. It happens sometimes with pneumonia. It wasn't the first time for him. He'd been sick before."

"What made anyone think he hadn't died a natural death?"

"Well, it could have been natural," Mrs. Galotti said. "I'm not saying it wasn't. But he'd been improving, his temperature was down, his breathing was pretty normal by that time. You could tell when you saw Dr. Fowler that he was a wreck over this. He wouldn't say anything, of course. He was a very discreet man. But it troubled him that that little boy died. The parents were beside themselves. They blamed the hospital, and they blamed poor Hazel. It wasn't Hazel's fault, I can tell you that. And the hospital did what it was supposed to," she said loyally.

"Why did a rumor get started in the first place that he hadn't died a natural death?" I asked.

"Well, maybe it was because the parents couldn't believe that he could die after he seemed to be improving. Maybe the hospital was just looking for a scapegoat, you know, someone to blame it on, so the hospital and the doctor would be cleared."

"But they never blamed it on anyone," I reminded her. "There was no case. It never came to court."

"You're right," she said, her head bobbing as she thought it over. "But the woman with the accent, she never came back."

"She never came back to work at the hospital?"

"Not that I heard. She was off the next night, the night after the little boy died. And she was off the night after that. So there was nothing funny there. But then she called in sick the night she was supposed to come back."

"So she was gone three days in a row."

"That's right. And then she just never came back."

"Did she call and quit?"

"If she did, I never heard about it. I heard she just plain never came back." She leaned toward me and said in a lower voice, "And I heard something else. I heard she never cashed her paycheck. I heard the post office sent it back."

"So she didn't wait to be paid," I said.

"Didn't wait for anything. Let me tell you, there was a lot of talk when she didn't show up for work and didn't pick up her check. They sent someone out to her house, and the landlord said she'd moved out."

I could feel my skin prickle. "Did he say when she moved?"

"That day," Jane Galotti said. "The day the little boy died. He was sure of the date because she settled up for her room or apartment or whatever it was she lived in. Came home from the hospital, packed her bags, and moved out. Never left a forwarding address."

If I were looking for suspicious behavior, I certainly

had it. But maybe the poor woman was afraid that, being a foreigner, she might be accused wrongly. "Let's go back to the night the little boy died. Did anything happen while Hazel was having her lunch that might make someone think that the German woman was involved in the boy's death?"

"If you mean did anyone see her do something to kill him, I have to say no. But she was in his room."

"How do you know that, Mrs. Galotti?"

"My friend Mary Catherine was the night nurse on that floor for nearly a hundred years, or so it must've seemed sometimes, and she saw that woman in the little boy's room."

Maybe it was my friendship with Arnold Gold, a lawyer who truly believes in equal opportunity to defend oneself against charges, and maybe it was because I try to be fair-minded even when it isn't easy, but I found myself taking the poor woman's side since she wasn't there to set the record straight herself. "But isn't that the job of the night people? To check up on patients?"

"Well, yes."

"And you said that Hazel had let them know she was going down to the cafeteria."

"That's what Hazel told me, and I believe her."

"So why was that unusual, for that woman to be in a patient's room? Why would anyone think it strange?"

"Because Mary Catherine walked down the hall, and when she walked back the woman was still there. Because she was there when Hazel was out to lunch." Jane Galotti spoke with fierce determination. She believed the woman was a killer, and she wanted me to believe it, too. *And the boy was dead when she came back.*

"And a couple of hours later the woman went home, packed her bags, moved out of her apartment, and was never seen again. It's very compelling."

"It's the truth."

"Thank you, Mrs. Galotti."

She smiled. "Now if I could just think of her name."

"You've given me more than enough. But if it comes to you, here's my address and phone number. Call collect. I'd like to hear anything you can think of."

She had a beautiful smile. "It's been so nice having a young person come to visit. I hope you liked the brownies. You didn't eat many."

I had limited myself to one, showing more willpower than I thought I possessed. "They're wonderful. I'm trying not to eat too many sweets."

"Look at you. You have nothing to worry about. I'll put a few in a plastic bag, and you take them home for later."

"My husband will appreciate them. Thank you."

"And I'll call if I think of that name."

At that point, I wasn't sure what I would do with it.

15

I felt totally wiped out on the drive home. I had been going since morning, had neglected to eat lunch, had forgotten my milk, and I was tired and hungry and loaded with guilt. This baby inside me needed calcium and iron and vitamins, and all I had ingested since breakfast was cookies and a brownie, not an exemplary diet for anyone. I wasn't doing a very good job as a baby producer, and I had no one to blame but myself.

The trip was interminable, twenty miles longer than the reverse since Jane Galotti lived deeper in Connecticut than Evelyn Krassky. And it was emotionally longer because I now had all the information I was likely to get from the Connecticut end, and although I knew a lot more, including the likelihood of a thirty-year-old murder, I didn't see where any of it connected to a man who had skated on thin ice and broken through.

One big question in my mind was whether the man married to Carlotta French was the little boy who had presumably died twenty-eight or twenty-nine years ago. Dr. Windham had removed the child's eyes; he would have known that he was working on a dead body. But was it possible the German woman had not killed the child—a crime for which I could think of no motive—but substituted a dead body for a living Val Krassky? Would Hazel, the private nurse, really have known that the dead child and the living child were different? Had Dr. Fowler seen the dead child? Dr. Windham had, but he hadn't known him. All he had done was remove the eyes.

And if that little Krassky boy had lived, what had become of him? Was there some adoption scheme involved or had the nurse's aide taken him herself? My head was throbbing.

By the time I turned down Pine Brook Road and coasted by the Grosses' house, I was weary with looking at angles and possibilities that bore no fruit. Why does a woman kill a child she doesn't even know? What could she possibly gain from it? And if she hadn't killed the boy, why did she run?

As I began to turn up my driveway, I was startled to see a maroon van alongside the house. The builders! I had totally put them out of my mind. I backed out of the drive and parked at the curb, feeling the weight of knowing I would have constant companions in my home for the next who-knew-how-long. I had been salivating at the thought of dropping on my own bed in my own room and taking a short nap. Now I was reminded that my bed wasn't in my room anymore, and my room probably wasn't even much of a room. And I had company.

I walked up the front walk and picked up the mail, went inside the front door, which I didn't use very often, and glided by the answering machine with my head averted. There would be a call from Carlotta. I hadn't called her since I got home, promising she would hear from me today, but if I knew Carlotta, she wouldn't be able to wait for my call. I went up the stairs and looked inside my old bedroom. No one was there and the room, though empty, was largely intact. I went back down, out the back door, and around to the back of the house. The lawn behind the kitchen was a little ragged, and a sketchy frame for the addition was already in place. What looked like an acre of blue plastic covered the structure. Here I was investigating a man's disappearance for the better part of a week, still trying to put things together, and these men had, in less than one full day, erected a good piece of the frame for a two-story addition.

We all said hello and then good-bye; they were finishing up for the day and would be back tomorrow, bright and early. I waved them away, went back in the house, and collapsed on the sofa.

I didn't stay there long. I went to the refrigerator to pour myself a generous glass of skim milk and downed it so quickly that I completely bypassed the taste. That alleviated a small portion of guilt. Then I listened to the answering machine.

"Chris, this is Carlotta, Monday morning. Is anything happening? I'm going to call or visit the high school that Val went to. I'm going to try very hard to find someone who'll look up his address at the time he went there. Everyone in the Buffalo area knows about the lake accident, so it shouldn't be too hard to find a sympathetic soul to take pity on me. Call when you can." The machine told me the call had come in not long after I had left for Connecticut. Then I heard Carlotta's voice again. "Chris? It's Carlotta. I've got an address!" She sounded very excited. "I drove over to the house, but no one was home. It's one of those two-families that are all over the area. The owner usually lives in the downstairs flat, but no one answered either bell. Call when you get home."

Well, I was home and I had had my milk. I dialed Carlotta's number.

"Hello?" There was an eagerness in her voice, as if she had been waiting by the phone for me to call.

"Carlotta, it's Chris. I just got home. That's very good news that you found where Val lived."

"I wish I could have talked to someone. I took the names from the mailboxes. Maybe I'll call this evening. Have you found out any more about those people in Connecticut?"

"Quite a lot. I've just spent the day up there."

"Talking to the parents?"

"Not the parents, the other Krasskys. They're in-laws, and they put me in touch with a retired surgeon who knew all about the death of the little boy."

"Then he did die," she said with disappointment.

"Yes, he died. I can't say for certain that the child they buried was their own, but it looks as though it was. It also looks as though a nurse's aide may have murdered him."

"Murdered the child?"

"A lot of people thought so at the time, but they kept it very quiet. Don't ask me why she did it. I have no idea and no one else does. The suspect packed her bags and disappeared the day the child died."

"You think—my God—you think she took a live boy with her and left behind a dead one?"

"I don't know what to say, Carlotta. She just disappeared—cleared out her apartment, settled up her rent, didn't collect her last paycheck, and was never seen again."

"This is absolutely crazy."

"My feelings exactly. I don't know if there's anything

else I can learn up there. I think I've exhausted my leads."

"And yourself, too, probably."

I appreciated her concern. "That, too. What I'd like to find out is whether the woman who may have killed the little boy lived in that house in Buffalo. I need something to link your husband with that child, although I really can't tell you why. I keep asking myself where that will lead, and the answer seems to be that I'll find out when I find the link. If there is one."

"It still doesn't tell us who killed Matty on the ice," Carlotta said.

"No, it doesn't."

"Or where Val is now."

"No," I agreed, "it doesn't tell us that either. Maybe that address in Buffalo will help."

"Will you come back tomorrow after you teach your class?"

"I can't, Carlotta. I have laundry to do, I have papers to correct, I have a class to prepare for next week. And I think I'd like to talk to an old friend of mine who usually comes up with some interesting insights when I need them."

"Sorry. I'm being pushy."

"Don't apologize. Let me get back to you when I know what's going on."

"Thanks. And take it easy."

The last was easy. I got a load of laundry going and sat down with the paper. When I'd read enough of other people's problems, I reheated some leftovers for my dinner. The brownies from Jane Galotti had saved me. There would be something sweet for Jack when he came home from law school tonight. Just as the semester I was teaching was coming to an end, so was his, and not a moment too soon. He needed a breather before the summer semester started, some time away from the books, some dinners at home with his wife, who was missing him very much at that moment.

I kept my eye on my watch. The daily schedule at St. Stephen's Convent, where I spent fifteen wonderful years before leaving to become a layperson, was permanently imbedded in my brain. I wanted to talk to my friend Sister Joseph, the General Superior, after she finished dinner and before she was too tired to think. The nuns of St. Stephen's arise at five in the morning, and by evening they're ready for bed. By nine o'clock there's hardly a sound except for the late-nighters who are finishing their showers.

At seven-thirty I called. A voice I didn't recognize answered, and I asked for Joseph.

"Who's calling, please?"

"Chris Bennett."

"One moment, please."

I wondered, while I waited, if the voice was that of a novice. In these days of shrinking convents, a novice is almost a novelty. Most days my friend Sister Angela is on bells, but at night, I supposed, she was relieved.

"Chris, is it really you?"

"Joseph. Yes. How are you?"

"Enjoying our beautiful spring. We're going to have a vegetable garden near the Villa. This afternoon we paced it off and started turning over the earth."

"That sounds like hard work."

"Well, we think it'll be worth it. One of the local farms shut down last fall. They sold the land to a developer."

"How awful."

"That's how we felt. How many ripe tomatoes will we lose to those little houses? We decided to be aggressive and plant our own. The Villa nuns have taken it upon themselves to plant the seeds. I must say, those little seedlings are cute as can be."

I smiled. I had learned the same thing myself in our backyard. "Good for you."

"I hope this call means we'll get to see you."

"I'd like to. Would it surprise you if I told you I'm working on a fascinating case that makes no sense at all?"

"It wouldn't surprise me in the least. In fact, I think you've just whetted my appetite. I don't suppose you could meet me in New York on Wednesday?"

"Wednesday would be perfect. Are you going to the Chancery?"

"Not this time. I'm meeting Sister Cecelia. You remember that she's going to nursing school."

"I do remember. Shall I come to her apartment?"

"That would make things very convenient. How's two? I want to have lunch with Cecelia. I'm sure we'll be through by then."

I called Carlotta and told her the earliest I could fly to Buffalo would be Thursday, and I would let her know at least a day ahead. She was disappointed, but I assured her that taking the time to see Joseph would be well worth the delay.

When I got off the phone, I did something I don't do very often. I sat down in front of the television set, closed my eyes, and fell asleep.

At my class on Tuesday, we reviewed much of what we had studied during the spring semester. A paper was due the following week—that would give me plenty of work, I thought, hoping I had some answers to Carlotta's case by then—and the week after that was the final. I had the usual range of questions and problems from my students: Could they hand the paper in the day of the exam? (No.) What exactly did the assignment mean? (See me after class if no one else has the same question.) Would it be OK to hand in a paper that wasn't as long as the assignment, like half as long maybe? (No.) Do you need footnotes? (Yes.) And finally, Could I give you my paper today? (You bet!)

I had my usual pleasant meal in the college cafeteria, ending with a glass of skim, and then drove home to my builders and my preparation for next week, including reading the term paper I had just been given. Happily, and not unexpectedly, it was a clear *A*, and I hoped not the last.

The noise from the builders, hammering mostly, was unrelenting, and I looked forward to my trip into New York tomorrow to get away from it all.

Late in the afternoon Carlotta called. "I talked to the owner of the building where Val lived," she said. "Last night, but I didn't want to bother you."

"What did you find out?"

"Not much, I'm afraid. They bought the house twelve years ago, about half a dozen years after Val graduated from high school. They don't have any idea who lived there then."

"What about the tenant who was living there when they moved in?"

"They're new. The old tenant moved out several years ago, and it wasn't a German woman and her son. It was a family with three daughters."

"Then it isn't ours," I said. "Someone must have preceded them. We'll have to find the former owner or that former tenant and see what they remember."

"The former owners were an elderly couple who'd lived there for over forty years, and they went to a retirement home when they sold. I have their name, and the name of the home the new owner thinks is where they went. To tell you the truth, I'm a little afraid to call. What if they've died?"

I understood her reluctance. "Give me the information you have, Carlotta. I'll call the home and ask about them. Then, if one or both of them is alive, I'll call and see if I can arrange to meet them later in the week."

"When do you think you'll come back?"

"Let's say Thursday. I'm meeting my friend tomorrow afternoon."

"Get your laundry done?" Carlotta asked with a smile in her voice.

"All done. And I'm trying to blow away the dust, but with the builders, it's a thankless job."

"I'll call the airline and get you a ticket."

"Sounds good." I copied down her names and phone numbers and said good-bye. The difficult part was mine. I took a deep breath and called the retirement home.

"Good afternoon, Golden Days Retirement Home."

"I'm trying to reach Mr. or Mrs. Stanley Kazmarek."

"I'm afraid Mrs. Kazmarek has passed away. Who is this, please?"

"My name is Christine Bennett. I live in Oakwood, down near New York City. May I speak to Mr. Kazmarek?"

She took a second to consider. "I'll put you through."

It rang three times before being picked up. "Hello?" It was an old voice.

"Mr. Kazmarek, my name is Christine Bennett."

"Who?" he asked.

"Christine," I said, raising my voice. "Christine Bennett."

"Do I know you?"

"No, sir. I'm trying to find some people who lived in your old house."

"I don't live there anymore."

"I know that. But I thought you might remember the people who used to live upstairs."

"I remember them. Nice folks."

For a moment I considered asking my questions, but I decided to wait. Face-to-face always works better, especially when there's a hearing problem, which I sensed there was. "Could I come by on Thursday afternoon and see you, Mr. Kazmarek?"

"What for?"

"To ask you about the people who lived in your old house."

"They were nice people," he said.

I didn't feel very good about this. "Will you be home on Thursday afternoon?"

"I'm home every afternoon, except if I have to go to the doctor."

"Good. Then I'll come on Thursday. Is that all right?"

"Sure. Maybe you could bring me a piece of chocolate."

"I'd love to. See you Thursday."

"Don't forget the chocolate."

I promised I wouldn't. I hoped he wouldn't forget our appointment.

16

Joseph and I go way back. I was fifteen, orphaned and frightened, when Aunt Meg took me to St. Stephen's on a rainy night that I will never forget, to live and eventually to become a nun. My cousin Gene, her only child, retarded from birth and suffering a number of health problems, had become too much of a burden for her and Uncle Will to cope with, along with the added problem of my presence. I had known for some time I wanted to be a nun, but I was too young to enter a convent. However, St. Stephen's understood my aunt's and uncle's terrible dilemma and accepted me, giving me a sanctuary I didn't really want at that moment, but which I came to appreciate. And a large part of the reason was Sister Joseph, who took me under her wing and eventually became my spiritual director. I still consider her my closest friend, although we no longer see each other on a daily or even monthly basis.

So it was with great eagerness that I dressed on Wednesday morning for my afternoon meeting with Joseph and Sister Cecelia. I had known Cecelia during my years at the convent, and I admired her. She was in nurses' training now, preparing to bring her skills back to the convent when she graduated. It was a long time since

I had seen her, before my marriage, when I had been living in Oakwood only a few months.

I greeted the workmen, got the house in order, and put my suitcase out on my bed to prepare for the next trip to Buffalo. I wasn't feeling very optimistic about Stanley Kazmarek. If his memory failed, the only other source would be the tenants who had moved out, but the likelihood that they would have any clear recollection of people they might have met only once—and, it occurred to me, might not have met at all if the apartment were vacant when they first saw it—was very small. But you take what you can, and certainly, that birth certificate for Val had yielded much more information than I could have imagined when we first looked at it.

With my suitcase mostly packed, I went downstairs and had a light lunch, topping it off with milk. I had to buy some chocolate before I left for Buffalo tomorrow, and I wouldn't know till tonight when I was leaving, so today was the day to do it. I said good-bye to the builders, who seemed to be making enormous progress in framing the addition, and drove off, stopping at a pretty little shop that carried all kinds of candy that they made in their own kitchen in the back. I indulged in a pound of their milk chocolate chunks, which I thought should satisfy any craving. As soon as I was on my way, I began to have second thoughts. Maybe Mr. Kazmarek suffered from a disease that prevented him from eating sweets, and he asked people who didn't know about it to help him break the rules. Well, I would just have to make inquiries before I presented him with my gift, and if he couldn't eat it safely, Carlotta would have to help me out.

Sister Cecelia lived in a small apartment, over on the east side of Manhattan near the hospital where she was studying. I parked in a garage and walked around the block to make sure I wouldn't be early and disturb their conversation. At two I announced myself at the door and took the elevator up.

"Chris," Joseph said happily, standing in the hall and waiting for me as I stepped off the elevator. "You look wonderful. We've been waiting for you to have some tea and hear your story."

"It's quite a story. Cecelia, it's good to see you after so long. How's nursing coming along?"

"Cecelia is getting an *A* average," Joseph said with pride. "We couldn't ask for more. I'm afraid someone will steal her away when she's through."

"No chance of that," Cecelia said. "I really can't wait to get back to St. Stephen's. I miss it terribly."

We sat at her kitchen table while they had tea, and we all talked about old times and mutual friends. When the tea and talk were done, Cecelia excused herself.

"Now that Joseph knows I'm getting straight *A*'s, I have an image to protect. If you don't mind, as much as I'd like to hear about your fascinating murder, I'm going to my room and hit the books."

When she was gone, Joseph said, "She's doing wonderfully. I think this is something she's wanted to do all her life, and now that it's happening, she couldn't be happier. But she does miss the community."

"I'll drop by when I'm in the city," I said. "I'll enjoy seeing her."

"That would be very nice, Chris. Now, I've got my pen and paper handy, and I'm ready."

I began with my first meeting with Carlotta French in February, about a week and a half after the Valentine's Day accident. I had my notebook open, my chronology in front of me, all the questions, all the answers, all the things that just didn't make sense. I went through it all, conscious that Joseph was taking notes. She stopped me a few times to ask a question and then told me to continue before I lost the flow of the narrative.

Finally, I turned my last page and looked up. "Tomorrow, I'm flying back to Buffalo, and the first thing I'll do is interview the man who owned the house where Val lived as a high-school student. I have no idea where I'll be going after that."

"Nor do I," Joseph said, "but you were right. This is certainly fascinating. An apparent drowning after what seems like a reckless trek across a frozen lake, and you've uncovered a possible thirty-year-old murder. Amazing."

"Why was that child killed, Joseph?" I asked.

"Something is tickling my brain. Let it stew awhile and I'll come back to it. Tell me again about the red scarf that was found on the ice."

"Carlotta said she and Val had given it to Matty for Christmas because he was a hunter, and I gather hunters have to wear red so they're not mistaken for deer."

"So the scarf belonged to the man who was shot."

"That's right."

"Next thing. You said that one of the wives—one of the widows, as it turns out—had a funeral for her husband before the bodies surfaced."

"That was Bambi Thayer, Clark's wife. I asked her about it. She said she knew he had drowned, and she wanted to go through the service at the time of his death."

"But Carlotta was sure that her husband was still alive?"

"She felt that Val was too smart to walk across the ice, that he wouldn't have taken that kind of chance."

"And the other one, Annie Franklin, what did she think?"

"She thought Matty had drowned with the others, but she waited till his body appeared to have a funeral. I gather Matty was the kind of guy who loved a challenge, and it sounded as though Clark could have been talked into doing almost anything that Matty wanted him to."

"But not Val."

"Not if you believe Carlotta." I looked at her. "Joseph, how much do we really know about what another person thinks?"

"Very little, when we see how wrong people can be about each other."

"I've known you more than half my life and there are many things I anticipate in how you act, how you respond, what your concerns are, but you continue to surprise me. You're not completely predictable any more than anyone else is. Sometimes, just when I expect you to utter a certain phrase, something entirely different comes out of your mouth. Carlotta believes that her husband didn't walk across the lake because that's what she wants to believe about him. It fits her image of the man she married, the man she wants him to be."

Joseph put her pen down, clasped her hands, and rested her chin on them for a moment. Then she looked across the small table at me. "What if Jack were having dinner with two old friends on a winter's night near Lake Erie, and one of the others suggested walking across the lake? Would he go? Could he be persuaded to go?"

That stopped me because I saw myself in Carlotta's position. "Not today," I said. "Ten years ago, I think he would have taken the dare. Maybe even five years ago. But not now."

"You mean he's grown up."

"He's grown up, he has me to come home to, he's in law school. He sees himself differently from five or ten years ago."

"But you can't be sure."

"Of course I can't be sure. And if I were out of town and they were very persuasive—" I didn't like to think about it. Here I was admitting it was possible, while Carlotta was absolutely sure. Val could not have joined them. Val wasn't crazy. "But I take your point. No matter how sure Carlotta is that Val didn't go, she could be wrong. His body may turn up tomorrow."

"With or without a bullet hole," Joseph said.

"I didn't think of that."

"And if it's without, we still don't know who killed Matty." She wrote something that she finished with a question mark. "Let's see what we have and then let me ask you some questions. Two or three men took a walk across Lake Erie and two or three had an accident, probably during a shooting incident, and fell into the lake and drowned. A red scarf belonging to Matty Franklin was found on the ice the next day. One wife immediately had a funeral for her husband, the other didn't. Nothing happened for three months, when two bodies surfaced, Matty's with a bullet. Am I right that no weapon was found?"

"Right."

"This is the point that you entered the picture. You learned that the men discussed the trek over dinner, but that neither Matty nor Clark returned home, presumably to give either an opportunity to get a gun. Meaning that one of them had it with him, or that Val was the man with the gun.

"Looking at other things, you discovered three bank accounts with over ninety thousand dollars in each one, all of them in Val's name alone. You learned that Val had secretly written a will, but the lawyer will disclose none of its provisions because there is no proof that Val is dead. In following up on Carlotta's theory that Val has gone off to hide with old friends, you checked a year's worth of telephone bills and found only business calls made by him. In other words, if there were people outside his milieu whom he kept in contact with, he didn't do it by telephone."

"That's the way it looks."

"He seems to have had a good relationship with his business partner, and I gather no one has come calling for the repayment of old debts."

"No one that Carlotta has told me about."

"But you've uncovered two rather mysterious facts: a million-dollar life insurance policy with Matty Franklin as the beneficiary, and a birth certificate in Val's name that records the birth of a child who seems to have died almost thirty years ago at the age of six or seven. We still don't know any more about that policy, do we?"

"No," I said. "I can tell you it was a shock to Carlotta and she's really angry about it. But no one will ever collect unless there's proof that Val died before Matty."

Joseph smiled. "Carlotta probably considers it money thrown away, and I would imagine the premiums were rather a lot of money every year. A million dollars may not be what it used to be, but it's still a hefty sum. All right. The other mystery is Val's birth certificate and everything you've dug up in Connecticut. It would seem that we don't really know whether Val is the person whose birth is recorded on the certificate. If he is, it appears that he didn't die of pneumonia at age six, but was somehow hustled out of the hospital by a devious woman who kept him as her son, eventually moving to Buffalo—why Buffalo?—where he went to school. And if that child did die, as seems likely from what the surgeon told you, then what?"

"That's what I'm here for, Joseph. A few good answers to a few good questions."

"I don't have any answers, Chris, good or bad. What I do have is some work for you, besides what you'll do tomorrow in Buffalo when you interview the owner of that house. Let me tell you what's been tickling my brain since you brought up the birth certificate.

"I have heard—and if I have, I'm sure many knowledgeable people have—that people trying to change their identity for whatever reason have been known to go to a cemetery and find the name of a person of the same sex and a similar age and assume that person's identity."

"I've heard about that, too," I said. "I gather if you write for a birth certificate, there's a good chance you'll get it because there's no cross-referencing of births and deaths."

"Which is not surprising. A person born in New York may die in Hawaii. Birth certificates aren't issued by the federal government but by local governments. I suppose one day all this will be computerized, along with everything else, and all the great mysteries of life will disappear, but until that time this kind of deception is available to anyone with a stamp.

"Now let's look at this woman who was seen in the little boy's hospital room about the time he died. She was not American-born. Several people noticed an accent. Whether it was German or French or Russian may be important later, but for the moment what strikes me as important is that she was not native-born. Let us suppose she has a son, a little boy about four or five or six years old. Maybe she left him behind in the old country; maybe she had him with her, perhaps illegally. She goes to work in a hospital, taking a night job when there are fewer people around to observe her when she takes a break or goes to lunch. What she's looking for is a record of the death of a boy about the age of her own child."

"Joseph, this is very disturbing."

"Disturbing, but is it outrageous from the point of view of reasonableness?"

I shook my head. "Go on."

"Maybe she can't find exactly the documentation she wants; maybe the records are locked up at night. Maybe she finds something but it isn't quite right. And then there's another possibility—no, let me leave that. One night while she's on duty, the perfect child is brought onto her floor with a medical problem that is potentially fatal. Perhaps the child even looks like hers."

"Joseph, this is terrible."

"Yes, it is. It's dark and ugly, but from what you've told me, I think something dark and ugly may have happened in the life of Valentine Krassky who did or did not cross Lake Erie on Valentine's Day."

"So you think this nurse's aide murdered the Krassky boy and transformed her son into Valentine Krassky."

"I think it's possible."

"Then really all she needed was the fact that the boy was dead and the information on his medical chart."

"Which probably contained his parents' names, their

address, maybe even the hospital the boy was born in if he was born in that same hospital."

"He probably was," I said. "They were living in the same house. They didn't move until after the hospital settled with them."

"So instead of waiting for the perfect child, this woman produced one."

"I think I will have a cup of tea," I said, somewhat defiantly. I poured for both of us, squeezed a little lemon in mine, and sipped it. "She had to get away from Connecticut, didn't she?"

"I would think so. She couldn't chance putting the boy into a local school where someone would recognize the name."

"If this is true, I wonder whether Val had any inkling of it."

"We'll never know if he doesn't turn up alive. And even if he did, Chris, he's in no way to blame for what his mother may have done."

"What a terrible secret," I said.

"If true," Joseph reminded me.

"And if it's true, does it connect with what happened on the lake that night almost thirty years later?"

"That may be the harder question. But I have some suggestions which will mean some additional work." She looked down at the pages she had filled during our talk. "I know that the hospital records are closed to you, but I think you might go back to Connecticut and walk through the cemetery where the original Val Krassky is buried."

"What am I looking for?"

"I'm not sure, but I would take a look at the names and dates on the tombstones."

"OK." I made a note, wondering when I would have time to get back there.

"And then you should think about the wife who made the funeral and the wife who didn't make the funeral. In fact, find out what you can about both wives."

"All right."

"And now I'm going to ask a question that I think nobody has asked so far because it sounds almost foolish. You know the old children's riddle: 'Why did the chicken cross the road?' And the answer is always: 'To get to the other side.' I think the assumption, and very likely the correct assumption, about why those three men walked across the ice to Canada is reflected in the old joke. But maybe it isn't. Maybe you could ask the question: 'Why did they cross the lake to Canada?' "

"It was a narrow strip," I said, giving her an answer she didn't want, "the shortest distance between two points. They could cross the border without going through customs. It was a lark."

"Perhaps it was." Joseph moved a page and looked at another. "Those phone bills you checked. Carlotta was able to identify all the people Val called, is that right?"

"Yes, and none were likely 'safe houses' for him. They were business associates. He didn't spend a lot of time on the phone with old buddies, and he had no relatives that she knew of. Also, there were no calls attributable to him after Valentine's Day."

"We wouldn't expect his mother to stay around if she had killed a child."

"Hardly."

"But in any case, Carlotta checked out people across the country."

"She did," I said. "Mostly her friends, but she checked after he disappeared."

"Chris, there are other ways to make phone calls if you don't want your wife to know you're making them."

I stared at her. People put calls on the same credit cards they use to buy clothes and meals with. As a person who has been unrelenting in not wanting to possess a credit card, I sometimes forget that most of the world is not like me. "I'll check that," I said.

"And then there's the red scarf," Joseph said. "It makes me wonder. How did the red scarf manage to get on the ice?"

"I think we all assumed that it was used by one person to help another stay out of the water."

"Unsuccessfully."

"Unfortunately."

"Then why didn't it go down with the drowning man?"

I had no answer. "He would have clung to it, wouldn't he?"

"It seems to me that would be the instinctive thing to do, to hang on to the lifeline, even after the other person let go or was dragged into the water himself. Something about that scarf troubles me, Chris. Did Matty toss it to one of the other men as he started to go down? Did neither of the others pick it up, and it just lay on the ice the rest of the night? Or did something else happen, perhaps something very sinister that no one has thought of, that caused the death of those two men and perhaps the third?"

"Involving the scarf?"

"Yes, somehow."

"I'll see what I can find out," I said.

Joseph smiled and moved the papers off to one side. "Now, what can you tell me about the Brooks family?"

"Well," I said, knowing that this was the moment, "it's expanding. I'm pregnant, Joseph."

"That's wonderful, Chris. I couldn't want better news. Then this may be your last case for a long time."

"I rather think so. I'd like to continue teaching if I can find a suitable sitter. It's only one morning a week, and I think it'll be good to keep my own life going. And maybe I can continue doing some work for Arnold at home. But another case? I don't really see how I could."

"Whatever you decide, I know it'll be the right thing. And I'm very pleased. May I tell the sisters?"

"Of course."

She looked at her watch, a serviceable stainless steel case with a large, round face. "I took the luxury of driving in. I think I'd better get going before everyone else in New York starts for home."

"Let's walk together. My car is around the corner."

By chance we were in the same garage. I let Joseph get her car first. Then I retrieved mine and started for home, Matty's red scarf waving in the back of my mind.

17

It was too late in the day to think about dashing off to Connecticut to walk around the cemetery. Cemeteries close about five o'clock, and it would take the better part of two hours to get from Manhattan to where I had been on Monday. So I drove home and arrived in time to say good-bye to my builders.

There was a message from Carlotta on the answering machine, and I called her back right away. A ticket would be waiting for me at La Guardia, and she would be at the Buffalo airport to meet me. We were on.

When Jack came home from his law school classes, we sat at the kitchen table, and while he ate, I told him about my afternoon with Joseph.

"For a woman who looks on the bright side of life, Sister Joseph sure picks up on the dark and ugly," he said.

"But it looks like she may be onto something. I'd been thinking about the switching of a dead body for a live one, about kidnapping the living child, about some crazy adoption scheme, all that kind of stuff. It was messy, and there were so many loose ends that I couldn't put together. What she suggested may be right. And there aren't many loose ends."

"Except what, if anything, it has to do with three guys crossing a frozen lake thirty years later."

"Maybe there isn't any connection, Jack. If you took a person at random and looked into his past, you might find out all sorts of pleasant and unpleasant things about him."

"Baggage."

"Right. And it might have nothing to do with whether he mows his lawn or screams at his kids."

"Sounds like you're arguing the opposite side. You're usually telling me how much our history is a part of our present."

I waved it off. "Just showing you I can go either way. Maybe nothing's there. It isn't really the crossing of the lake; it's the bullet in Matty. If those men had just fallen through the ice, it would be an accident. Something else happened; that's what makes this so interesting. I hope this Mr. Kazmarek tells us something useful tomorrow."

"Get him his chocolate?"

"A whole pound. Want a piece? I'm starting to think a pound of chocolate may not be the best thing for an old man to eat."

"No thanks. Gotta watch my midsection. I don't want my kid to think I'm fat."

I got up from the table and kissed him on my way to the sink. I hadn't even felt the baby move yet, and it was changing our lives.

Carlotta met me at the same time and the same place at the Buffalo airport, and we went downstairs to the luggage area like veterans. From there we drove to a restaurant in suburban Buffalo for lunch. The retirement home that Stanley Kazmarek lived in was also on the outskirts

of the city, and by the time we got there, it was just about
two. I wasn't sure whether he would even remember that
we had an appointment.

There was a front desk with a phone board and what
looked like a computer screen, and a woman with a smile
waiting for us.

"I'm here to see Stanley Kazmarek," I said.

"Oh, yes. He did say he was expecting a lady. You can
go right up. It's number three-C."

"I've brought him some chocolate. Do you know if he
has any dietary restrictions?"

"Let me check with the dietician." She dialed a
number and held a brief conversation. "She says he's
sound as can be, but no one should overindulge."

I considered that a message to me. "I'll tell him you
said so."

"Thanks for asking."

We went upstairs and rang his doorbell. I could hear
him inside, singing something I couldn't recognize.

Suddenly the door was pulled open. "Yeah," he said.

"Mr. Kazmarek, I'm Christine Bennett. We talked on
the phone the other day."

"Was that you who called?"

"Yes, it was. This is my friend, Carlotta French."

"You from the insurance company?"

"No, sir. We're trying to find the people who used to
live in your house in Buffalo."

"Sure, sure. Come in. You got something for me?" His
eyes were sparkling in anticipation. He was a paunchy
man, not much taller than I. He wore a pair of corduroy
pants, a gray shirt with no tie, and a very rumpled jacket
that was missing a button. We followed him into a small
living room that could not have accommodated many

more guests and sat on a sofa just big enough for two. He plumped into a worn chair that faced the television set.

"I brought you some chocolate, Mr. Kazmarek."

He leaned forward for it. "I like chocolate. I don't get much anymore. Not since my wife died."

I wondered whether he was aware that you could buy it for yourself. "Mr. Kazmarek, do you remember the people who rented the upstairs flat when you owned your house?"

He ignored me. He peered into the bag with its foil lining, then pulled out a chunk of chocolate. His lips moved into a smile. He took a bite out of it with difficulty, then sat back and enjoyed it. Carlotta and I watched. He never offered us any, never thanked us, never even acknowledged that we were there. He seemed transported to another place. Finally, he folded down the top of the bag and set it aside.

"Who did you say you were?" he asked, his forehead wrinkled in a questioning frown.

"I'm Chris Bennett. This is Carlotta French. We're trying to find the people who rented the flat above yours in the house you owned."

"The one over by Starin?"

"That's the one."

"Nice house," he said. "Big rooms. We raised our kids there. This place is so small." He looked around claustrophobically. "I still think we shouldn'ta moved but my wife, she said it was too much to take care of and she didn't want the responsibility."

"The people upstairs," I said. "Do you remember them?"

"Yeah. They had a bunch of girls. One of them had a nice voice. She used to sing all the time."

"Do you remember who lived there before that family moved in?"

"Before the one with the girls?"

"Yes."

He made a face, trying to remember. "There was some folks lived there a long time. What was their name? Had a boy and a girl, I think."

"Do you remember their name?"

"With an L. Lit—, Lip—, Lish—. I wish I could remember it. Lipchinski! That's it. They were the Lipchinskis."

I wrote it down, as near as I could spell it. "A husband and wife?" I asked.

"A whole family, the mother, the father, the sister, the brother."

"Was the boy's name Val?"

"Val?"

"Yes, like Valentine."

"A boy named Valentine?"

"Yes."

"Never heard of him. The Lipchinski boy was a name like John. Nice boy. Terrible thing, what happened to him."

I could feel Carlotta tense. "What happened to him?" I asked.

"Went into the army after high school. Got killed in an accident. I remember it like it was yesterday." He seemed sure of himself now. "We went to the funeral, Mary and me. Funny you should bring that up. I haven't thought of that boy for years."

I gave him a minute to work through his memories. "Maybe the people I'm looking for were before the Lipchinskis," I said, knowing that I was going back too far.

"Before them? There wasn't anybody before them."

"About twenty years ago," I said, picking a time when Val would have been in high school.

"Twenty years ago? What am I now—eighty-three?"

"About that," I said.

"So I was sixty. I don't remember. Besides, the Lipchinskis lived there when we bought the house. That boy was born there. If my wife was alive, she could tell you all about it."

I felt a wave of disappointment pass through me. He seemed to know what he was talking about. If he had a name or date slightly wrong, he was still doing well. "Mr. Kazmarek, there was a boy who went to Bennett High School about twenty years ago and he gave your address as his home."

"My house?"

"Yes."

"You don't mean John?"

"No, not John."

He shrugged his shoulders. "I don't know. You think they had company living with them or something?"

"Do you remember that?"

Suddenly his face brightened. "I know what you mean. You mean that crazy bunch who lived in the attic."

"There were people living in the attic?"

"We fixed it up. We thought maybe we could use the space. Put a bathroom up there and everything."

Carlotta, who had not said a word since we sat down, put her hand over mine.

"Do you remember who lived there?" I asked.

"A woman and a coupla boys. It wasn't legal, that apartment. You're not gonna get me in trouble, are you?"

"Not at all. I'm not interested in the apartment. I'm

interested in the woman and the boys. Do you remember their names?"

"Nah. My wife could tell you. She handled all that. I kept out of the way."

"What did the woman look like?" I asked.

"Stout, gray hair pulled back in a bun. Heavy accent. I couldn't make head or tail of what she said. Mary took care of it. Mary took care of everything," he said sadly.

From chocolate to tenants, I thought. "Do you remember the boys' names?"

"Never knew 'em. Sometimes they were there, sometimes they weren't."

"What do you mean?"

"They would go away somewheres. Don't ask me where. They just picked up and left on Friday, came back on Monday. They were a crazy bunch. No father, no mother."

"I thought you said there was—"

"An old woman. Leastways she looked old, too old to be their mother. I don't know. How old do I look to you?"

"You look like you're in good health, Mr. Kazmarek," I said, not wanting to get into a guessing game. "I wouldn't think you're as old as you said."

"What did I say? Eighty-three?"

"That's what you said."

He looked inside the bag again and broke off another piece of chocolate. I started to get nervous. "Good stuff," he said. "My wife used to get me chocolate all the time. She used to bake chocolate cakes for me. Nobody does that anymore."

"I'm glad you're enjoying it. I hope you save some for later."

"Oh, sure. Save a little for later."

"Would you remember the name of that old woman if you heard it?" I asked.

"I might."

"Was it Krassky?"

"Krassky?"

"Yes."

"Never heard of it."

"Do you know what country she was from?"

He shrugged.

"How long did she live there?"

"Coupla years. My wife could tell you exactly. She kept the records."

I wanted to ask if they had left a forwarding address, but I knew it was hopeless. "Were they good tenants?" I asked instead, just to see if I could get him to talk about them.

"They paid on time. That's all I cared about. The boys made some noise running around. The Lipchinskis complained, but the Lipchinskis made their own noise. Ain't much you can do about noise."

I turned to Carlotta. "I guess that's it. Anything you want to ask?"

"What did the boys look like?"

"Big," he said. "Like football players. Polite, too. Always nice to me and my wife."

"Do you think one of them could have been named Val?"

"Could be," he said. "But I couldn't swear to it."

Even if he had sworn to it, I would have been skeptical. We shook his hand and left.

18

"Val really lived there," Carlotta said, as we walked out to the car. "We've really found a place in the past that we can tie to him."

"But we don't have a name, and since the apartment was illegal, there's no record anywhere that they ever lived there. And the nurse I spoke to in Connecticut said the aide who was suspected of killing the child was thirty or thirty-five. Even if she was off by five or six years, a sixty-year old man wouldn't call her old ten years later."

"Maybe she just gained weight, dressed like a frump, and had graying hair."

"I suppose so," I said without conviction.

"I wish his wife were still alive. She'd probably remember everything that ever happened."

"It looked that way, didn't it? It's funny how dependent he was on her. He probably thinks his clothes wear out because she died."

"They probably do. Val and I have always been very independent. He goes out and buys his shirts and ties without help. It's one reason I can't tell you if anything's missing."

"Carlotta, there are a few things I want to check that my friend suggested to me yesterday. She thinks it's odd

177

that Bambi had a funeral before Clark's body was found."

"So do I. But the police were sure all three men were dead. They said as much."

"I also find it hard to believe that Matty didn't leave any address for his mother. Annie said she lived in England and they weren't in contact with each other. Even if they'd had a falling out, wouldn't he have some way of reaching his own mother?"

"Val didn't," Carlotta said shortly.

"He must have known, then. Somehow he must have found out that his mother was a killer, and he severed his relationship with her. It's too weird. We're still missing a lot of pieces. Tell me, who paid the credit card bills in your family?"

"Val did. He had software on his computer where he could tick off the deductibles, so I just turned everything over to him."

"Then you never saw his bills?"

"There wasn't any need to."

"Let's take a look when we get home. He may have made phone calls and charged them to credit cards. If he knew you never looked at his charges, it was a safe way to keep them secret from you."

"I hate the idea of his keeping secrets."

"You want to find him, don't you?"

She nodded. "I know where the records are. We'll look when we get home."

By the time we got there it was late afternoon. Carlotta went directly to Val's office and opened a drawer in his filing cabinet. She pulled out a folder marked TAXES and gave it to me.

"This is how he did it," she said. "When a bill was

paid, he chucked it into the folder. At the end of the year, when it was complete, he went through it if he had to. Things may be grouped into categories like mortgage payments, utilities, gasoline, and that kind of thing. I really don't know. I took the file for last year and gave it to our accountant without looking at it. It was just too painful. The telephone bills that you looked through are all there. After Val disappeared, nothing was added to the computer records, but this is all the raw data."

I took it and sat down with the folder on my lap. I took a quick look at this year's pre-Valentine's Day bills. There was almost nothing. January bills would have come in February. One telephone bill went through the beginning of February, and I had looked at that on my last visit. But there was also an American Express bill and a couple of other credit card bills. I went over every item and found no phone calls.

Then I started looking at last December and earlier. Month after month, bill after bill listed no phone calls. If he charged calls, he made them with a telephone credit card and they all appeared on his monthly statement. There was nothing here to help me.

I suddenly felt frustration that bordered on anger. I needed a name. Mr. Kazmarek had given me nothing except an indication that Val could have lived at his address twenty years ago. If the people in the attic had a telephone, and I assumed they did, it could have been in any name in the book. If the woman had moved, she was untraceable without a name. For all I knew, she might still live in Buffalo, and Val might have called her daily without a toll charge. He might have visited her on his lunch hour. She and I might have brushed shoulders on the street, and how would I know?

I found Carlotta sitting in her family room. "Maybe Mr. Kazmarek's neighbors lived there twenty years ago and would remember the woman and her sons who lived in that attic."

"I hadn't thought of that." She looked at her watch. "Do you want to go now?"

"It's too late. People don't like to open their doors after dark. Let's do it in the morning."

"First thing," she said with determination.

"How's the morning sickness?" Carlotta asked as I stepped into the breakfast room the next morning.

"Manageable," I said. "Being vertical helps. Getting something inside me helps, too."

"How shall we do it this morning? You take one side of the street, I'll take the other?"

I paused just long enough that she caught my hesitation.

"You don't want me?"

I laughed. "Don't put it that way, Carlotta. I just think having two people canvassing a block is not the cleverest way to go. I'll do it myself and come right back here as soon as I know something."

"I'll drop you off," she said. "It's too long a drive to go back and forth. But I promise I'll stay out of your way."

We drove into Buffalo, and Carlotta worked her way through the city to a commercial street called Hertel Avenue. She turned a corner, and we were in a totally residential area. Everything was low, as though high-rise apartment houses were unheard of. There were one-family and two-family houses on quiet streets, narrow driveways hinting at the size of cars when these houses had been built. It was quiet and pleasant, a nice place to raise a family, a place where you could literally walk to the grocery and pick up a container of milk. I was in a big city with a very small-town atmosphere, and it made me feel comfortable and at home.

"The house is halfway down this street on the right," Carlotta said, stopping at a corner. "Shall I come by for you in an hour? Half an hour?"

"It's hard to judge. It depends on how many people are home and how many of them remember twenty years ago. Why don't you come back at thirty-minute intervals?"

"OK. And if you don't see me, look for me at this corner."

"See you later."

I got out of the car and walked down the street where the Kazmareks had lived for the largest part of their lives. I stayed on the far side of the street so I could look across and get a picture of the house. Once I saw it, I could see the larger windows on the third level, different from the other similar houses on the block. I knew that many homeowners in New York built illegal apartments in their basements or behind the unmoving doors of a built-in garage for extra income that was also tax free, often providing the difference between getting by and having to give up the house.

I crossed the street and rang the downstairs doorbell of the house to the right. No one answered. I rang the upstairs bell.

"Who is it?" an older female voice called from the second floor.

"My name is Chris Bennett. I wanted to ask you about the people who lived next door to you."

"I haven't seen them in ten years," she called back.

"Did you know the Kazmareks?" My voice was getting a little worn out, but she would not come downstairs and I didn't blame her.

"Yes, but they moved out a long time ago."

"Mrs. Martone," I called, reading her name off the mailbox, "I want to ask you about some people that lived in the Kazmareks' house about twenty years ago."

There was a silence. Then, "Oh, all right. Just a minute and I'll come down."

I waited at the top of the five steps in the entry hall. A few minutes passed. Then, through the curtain on the small window in the door, I could see a figure descending the stairs. The door opened and a gray-haired woman in a loose housedress came out.

"What was your name?"

"Christine Bennett. Chris."

"I'm Betty Martone." She closed the door to her flat. "Why don't we just talk down here? I don't like to have strangers upstairs."

"Here is fine. Did you know the Kazmareks?"

"For years and years. She's dead now. He lives out Main Street somewhere in an old folks' home. I'm not sure he's all there anymore."

"Mrs. Martone, I'm trying to find someone who lived in their house about twenty years ago, more or less. He would have been a teenager then, and I think he lived in the attic apartment. "

"Oh, that attic!" She gathered her skirt together and sat on the top step. Following her example, I sat a foot or so away so that we could look at each other. "Let me tell you about that attic. They were nice people, Stanley and Mary, but they went too far with that attic. You know, if you're going to make a three-family house, you've got to go downtown and file the papers. The neighbors can have their say, too. Who wants a street full of three-families? I didn't. Most of the other folks on the block didn't. So they just plain bypassed us. They said they were building another bedroom up there that they could use as a den. But who lives on the first floor and has a den on the third? It was ridiculous from the start." She sounded as though she were fighting the battle all over again. "And then, as soon as the last nail was hammered in, what do you suppose they did?"

"They rented it out," I said, hoping the lesson in real estate would not continue much longer.

"That's just what they did, they rented it out to a woman that had no husband and a couple of boys that were in and out all day long."

"Did you know them?"

"Said hello to her in the street once or twice. She wasn't the friendliest person I ever met."

"Was she the mother of the boys?"

"Oh, I don't know. Maybe, maybe not."

"And there were two boys?"

"It looked like twenty sometimes. But I think there were two."

"Did they have a lot of company?"

"Didn't have any. I don't think anyone ever went up there. But they were in and out all the time. They'd go away on Friday and come back on Sunday night. Holidays, they'd go away."

"Did she speak English?" I asked.

Mrs. Martone looked at me. "Well, now that you mention it, I think she had an accent."

"Did you happen to know her name?"

"Never knew it."

"The Kazmareks never mentioned it?"

She laughed. "We weren't on the best terms with Stanley and Mary during those years. My husband just wanted them out. Imagine people living in an attic. It gave the street a bad name."

"I know just what you mean," I said, agreeing with her to keep our relationship friendly. "How long did they live there?"

"Well, a bunch of us got together and told Stanley if he didn't get rid of them, we'd go to city hall and make a stink."

"So he threw them out?"

"He said he'd make them go as soon as the school year was over, and he did."

"Did you ever hear the boys' names?"

"Probably, but it's a long time ago." She looked at her watch. "I really can't sit here and blab all day. I haven't been much help, have I?"

"Not at all. You've been very helpful. Do you know anyone on the block who might have known the boys?"

She pursed her lips and looked out the front door. "Zimmerman on the other side, a couple of doors down. They had sons. They're all grown and gone now, but I think those boys played with the ones in the Kazmareks' attic."

"Zimmerman," I repeated.

"About three doors down to the right."

"Thank you, Mrs. Martone. You've been very helpful."

19

I walked back to the corner to see if Carlotta was waiting, but there was no sign of her car, so I went back down the street two doors past the Kazmareks' house. The inside foyer was identical to the one I had just visited: five steps leading up to two doors, on the right-hand wall at the bottom two mailboxes, one marked Black, one marked Zimmerman. Zimmerman was upstairs. I rang the doorbell.

"Yeah, I'm coming," a man's voice called from upstairs, and then his feet pounded down the stairs. "Yes?" he said, opening the door. He was in his sixties, fairly tall, wearing work pants with paint stains.

"Mr. Zimmerman?"

"You selling something?"

"No. I'm looking for someone who was a neighbor of yours before he moved away."

"Who's that?"

"The family that lived in the Kazmareks' attic."

"Oh, them. Yeah, I remember them. Been gone a long time. I couldn't tell you where they are."

"I understand your son knew those boys."

"I think he did. Yeah. They used to play over in the school yard."

"Do you remember those boys' names?" I asked.

"Too long ago, if I ever knew them. I could call my son. You wanna come up?"

I hesitated a moment, and he said, "My wife's upstairs. It's OK."

I followed him. His wife came into the living room and introduced herself, while he went to the kitchen and made a phone call.

"Is the fireplace real?" I asked, looking at the one built into the living room wall.

"Only for gas," Mrs. Zimmerman said. "It doesn't work anymore. I guess they kept a heater in there in the old days. These houses go way back."

"Flo?" her husband called. "Ask the lady to step in here. I've got Roger on the phone."

I went into the kitchen.

"Here's my son," Mr. Zimmerman said. "He's about your age. Talk to him."

I took the phone and told the man at the other end what I was interested in.

"Haven't thought of those folks for a long time," he said. "I don't have any idea what happened to them."

"Did you ever visit them at home?"

"No way. No one was allowed up there."

"Did the boys come to visit you?"

"She wouldn't have it. Sometimes they snuck in someone's house on the way home from school, but she kept a tight rein on them."

"Do you know her name?"

"Nope."

"What about the boys? Was one of them named Val?"

"Val," he repeated. "Gee, I don't know. It could be.

The one I knew was named Matty, Matty Franklin, I think."

Carlotta was parked around the corner, reading the *New York Times*. I got into the car, hardly knowing where to start.

"Matty lived in that attic," I said.

"Matty?"

"I talked to a man who was friendly with him in high school, but they never went to each other's houses because the mother, or whoever she was, wouldn't allow it."

"This is very crazy."

"Yes. I'm going to have to go back to that cemetery and see if there's a stone for Matthew Franklin."

"You think that woman killed another child?"

"I don't know. But if Val and Matty lived in the same house during high school, there's more than just an old friendship between them."

"And Val left a million-dollar life insurance policy to Matty. It starts to make sense now. I wonder if Matty left anything to Val."

"Annie might know."

"Annie might not tell you. Any more than I told Annie about the policy we found. We're in something very big, Chris. Who is my husband? Who is Matty?"

"I wish I knew."

"It's starting to look like there was something between Val and Matty that went sour, but I swear to you, Val didn't own a gun."

"Then maybe it was Matty's and there was a fight on the lake, and either Val or Clark got hold of it."

"Two against one and the gun went off."

"You realize you've just accepted the fact that Val was on the ice with the others."

"I haven't accepted anything. I've just presented a possible scenario. Listen to me. Scenario. I sound like a TV movie. Where do we go from here?"

I wasn't sure. "I still have several things I want to look into. How far are we from Bennett High School?"

"Not far. We can be there in five or ten minutes."

"Let's go."

She started the motor, drove back to Hertel Avenue and took it to Main Street. The school, a large red brick rectangle with an enormous number of stairs leading up to the front doors, was just down the street. Carlotta found parking on a side street, and we walked back to the school and up all the stairs. Inside, we found the office, just to the right of the door. I let Carlotta do the talking. On the way, I had sketched out a little script that I hoped would get us some information.

"I'm the wife of Val Krassky," she said to the pleasant woman who came over to help us. "He's one of the men who was in the accident on the lake in February."

"Oh, yes, I remember. I'm so sorry for you, dear."

"Thank you. We're trying to set up a fund in their memory and we haven't been able to find a high school address for Clark Thayer. Do you think you could look him up for me? He went to Bennett around twenty years ago, give or take a few years."

"Sure thing. Let me see what I can find."

It had occurred to me that no one remembered Clark, and the people I'd spoken to recalled only two boys living in the attic apartment. I wanted to know whether Clark was in any way a part of the group.

The woman went through several drawers, then left

the room. We looked at each other, but said nothing. I walked away from Carlotta and looked at the pictures on the wall, photographs of recent classes: eighteen-year-olds at the start of their adult lives, a football team, all the bodies identical and only the heads showing a hint of the individual within the padded shoulders.

A door opened and I went back to the counter. The woman who had been searching had returned.

"I'm awfully sorry, Mrs. Krassky. I can't find Clark Thayer's name anywhere. Are you sure he went to Bennett?"

"I thought he did," Carlotta said. "His wife told me— I'd better check with her."

"I'm really sorry I can't help you." She sounded very sincere.

"Thanks for your trouble."

We left the office and walked out of the building. "When I talked to Bambi, she told me he went to Bennett," I said.

"She must have gotten it wrong. They must have met some other way."

"How?" I asked. "They all went in different directions after high school."

"Well, maybe they were neighbors. Clark may have gone to a Catholic school. There are a lot of Catholic schools in Buffalo." She thought about it. "Bambi isn't Catholic, I'm sure of that. I think they went to a Protestant church together."

We went down the steps, crossed Main Street, and found the car, but we didn't get in. We stood on the street while I tried to think.

"The woman in the attic is a dead end," Carlotta said.

"I agree. Without a name, there's no way to trace her.

And for all we know, she used a false name. If she was trying to cover her tracks, why should she tell the truth? As long as you can pay a month's rent and a month's security, you can get an apartment, especially an illegal one."

"I'd like to know if Matty took out life insurance with Val as beneficiary."

"There's no way to find out. Annie won't tell you. If she found a policy the way you found yours, she'd be just as mad as you were. She'll cancel the policy if she can before she knows if Val is dead or alive. And what difference will it make if we find out that there is such a policy? Aside from the fact that it would be nice to inherit a million dollars, all it'll tell us is what we already know, that there's some strong bond between the two men."

"So where do we go from here?"

That was the question I was asking myself. "Something occurred to me this morning," I said. "There's a possibility that I overlooked something at the business. I'd like to see Jake again."

"I just don't understand what you think Jake has to do with all this. There's nothing there, Chris. It's wasted time."

Again her reluctance to have me talk to Jake, or was it to have me poke around the papers in Val's office? "Carlotta, we don't know what's wasted time until we explore. Who would have thought I would find out all that information in Connecticut on the basis of a birth certificate?"

"But you've talked to Jake. You've been through Val's papers. You said there was nothing."

"There's something I forgot."

She waited for me to say something else, to tell her

what I had forgotten, but I had no intention of giving her a reason to alert Jake. "Let's drive over there," I said, and we got in the car.

"I think I'll come in with you," she said, as she started the motor.

I was beginning to feel very uncomfortable, and it had nothing to do with morning sickness. "Carlotta, I'm doing this myself. If there's something that Jake knows that you don't want me to know, you should tell me about it now."

"There's nothing."

I didn't like it. This was the one person she had delayed in getting me to see, the one she visibly tensed up about when his name came up.

It passed through my mind that she and Jake had had something going at one time, either before or during her marriage. It wasn't the kind of information I looked forward to hearing, but, of course, it gave Jake a motive to be a killer. Although how Jake would have known about the trek across the lake was beyond me.

We drove in uncomfortable silence for several minutes. Then Carlotta said, "Whatever you're thinking, it didn't happen."

I tried not to smile. "I just want to follow up on something I forgot about last time."

"And you won't tell me what."

"I'll tell you when I find what I'm looking for—if I find it."

"Fair enough."

Jake seemed surprised to see me, which meant he had no idea I would be back. Better to catch him off guard, without time to shred and burn.

"I didn't know you were back in town," he said.

"I got in yesterday. I think we have to talk, Jake."

"About what? We talked last week. If I know more than I told you, I don't know that I know it."

"I want to know about relationships, about you and Carlotta."

"Me?" He smiled and his face relaxed. "Something between me and Carlotta? Hey, she's my partner's wife and I love her like a sister. If there's something between us, I'm the last guy to hear about it. You better ask her."

The way his face changed when I asked my question, the way his whole body untensed, I felt that I had hit a dead end. "Val and Annie," I said.

"I don't think so. They met years ago, I really don't remember how. I think she came to Buffalo for a job."

"Did they go out?"

"Yeah, they went out. It wasn't anything that produced sparks. When Annie saw Matty for the first time, that was explosive. I don't think either one of them ever looked at anyone else after that. They just clicked."

"Did anything happen between Annie and Val after she married Matty?"

"I just told you. Neither one of them ever looked at anyone else. Val included."

"There's one thing I forgot to ask you when I was here last week. Your telephone bills for last year. Could I see them?"

"My what?"

"Phone bills. I'd like to see if Val made any personal calls from this phone."

"They're not easy for me to put my hands on," he said. "Besides, you looked at his Rolodex, didn't you?"

"That's not the same as making calls."

"Everyone makes personal calls from work. I call my doctor, my lawyer, my wife about fifty times a day."

"Those aren't long-distance calls. I'm looking for long distance that isn't business-related."

"You know what you're in for? Matching up numbers on the bill with numbers on the Rolodex? It'll take you all day to do one month."

"I've got all day," I said, watching his growing agitation. "Can I just see the phone bills?"

He looked at a loss. "I don't know where they are. It'll take me some time to find them."

"You must have had them to prepare your taxes in April."

"Yeah, right." He scratched his head. "Look, I'm kind of busy right now. Could you come back later, or maybe on Monday?"

"Jake, this is what I'm here for. I can't sit around all weekend waiting for Monday."

"Let me see what I can find." He opened the door to the back area and went toward his office as I followed. He turned into it, and as I reached the doorway, he was dialing a number on the telephone.

"Couldn't it wait?" I said.

He slammed the phone down. "Who invited you in here?"

"I'm waiting for the phone bills."

He got up from the desk and went to a file cabinet, opened a drawer near the floor, and pulled out a thick file folder. He went through it as I waited, finally pulling out a rubber-banded pack of bills. "You want last year?"

"Last year'll be fine."

He started to toss the pack to me, but thought better of

it and handed it to me. He wasn't happy. "Where do you want to sit?"

"I'll go to Val's office."

"I shouldn't've given you those bills. The cops didn't even ask for them."

"The cops think he's dead."

"He is dead. Whatever his secrets, they should die with him. Whoever he called, it has nothing to do with you or Carlotta or Matty or Clark."

"Is this what Carlotta was afraid I would see?"

"I don't have any idea what Carlotta was afraid of. Excuse me, I have work to do."

I took the pack of bills to the office across the hall and sat down at Val's desk. The bills were addressed to the business and began with January of last year. I took the rubber bands off, divided the pack in two so they wouldn't fall all over the place, and began to go through the January pages. Many of the numbers called were in the same 716 area as the business, but were toll calls nevertheless. I didn't know what I was looking for, but when I turned the page, I saw that it had been made very easy for me. A small red check mark appeared next to a call that lasted seven minutes. The area code was 905. I wrote down the number, not sure why it was checked, but it was the only one on the page that was. Two pages later, another call was checked. It was to the same number. I flipped to the next checked call. Again it was to the same number. I picked up the phone on Val's desk and dialed the number. It rang three times, and a mechanical voice said the phone had been disconnected. Could it have been a business? Hardly, I thought. A business would have a forwarding number. This was a personal call, checked because Val was scrupulously honest. When I reached the last page of the month of January, his honesty was spelled out in red ink, the total cost of all the calls he had checked during the month. I felt excited by what I had found. I had no idea where the 905 area was, but someone at that number had gotten calls from Val on a regular basis.

I picked up the phone again and dialed the operator. "I wonder if you could tell me where area code nine-oh-five is," I said when she answered.

"That's Ontario," she said.

"Canada?"

"That's right."

"Thank you."

I hung up and as I did, one of the things Joseph had said to me, the thing she thought might sound strange, flashed into my head: *Where were the men going?* They were going to Canada, to Ontario, to be more exact, since that was the province on the other side of Lake Erie. And Val called someone in Ontario every few days during the month of January last year.

I grabbed February and started to run through the pages.

"So you found it," Jake said, as I returned to the outer area about half an hour after I had begun my search.

"Tell me about it."

"I know as much about those calls as you do."

"Is he the one who marked them in red?"

"With his own little red pen."

"Why?"

"Because they were frequent and personal and added up to twenty bucks or more a month, two hundred, maybe three hundred a year. He reimbursed the business for them. Val was that way. He didn't take anything for free."

"How long have they been going on?" My search of the bills showed the calls had been made through all of last year.

"Forever. Since he moved in with Carlotta. Maybe before that."

"You ever overhear a call?"

"No." The way he said it, he didn't want any further questions on that subject.

"Sure you did, Jake. You must have been curious."

"Look, he never made a call in front of me. He must have made them all from his office or when I was out of earshot. I couldn't tell you if they had to do with sex or money, whether he called a man or a woman."

"What?"

"I'm not suggesting anything. I'm just saying, he called someone, it was his business and he paid for the calls. End of story."

"How did he bring it up the first time?"

"You mean years ago? He said he had some personal calls he wanted to make during the day, and he'd pay for them at the end of the month. It was no big deal."

"But they went on until he disappeared."

"Until Valentine's Day. He made the last one that morning, before he left for lunch with Carlotta."

To say, *I'm coming tonight*? "And then the number was disconnected?"

"What?"

"I called it. It's out of service."

"Jesus." He looked upset. "You going to tell Carlotta?"

"Probably. She's the one who asked me to do the digging. You think she didn't know about the calls?"

"I'm sure of it."

So what was her problem? Why didn't she want me talking to Jake? "Just one more thing. I asked you about Val and Annie. What about Val and Bambi?"

"Shit," Jake said.

20

"So what did you find out?" Carlotta was standing near her car, which she had parked far enough away from the red brick building that Jake couldn't see her if he looked out the window.

"Two things. One you know and didn't tell me, the other you didn't know."

"Why don't you start with the one you think I don't know."

"Val made calls several times a week to a phone number in Canada."

"It was probably business."

"It wasn't. It was personal, and he reimbursed the business for them."

She swallowed, looking very unhappy. "Who was he calling?"

"I don't know. I dialed the number, but it's been disconnected."

"So what are you telling me? That he was involved in the international drug trade? That he had a girlfriend in Niagara Falls that he never saw, but he couldn't live without talking to?"

"I don't know. The last time he called the number was

on Valentine's Day, in the morning, before he took you to lunch."

"Chris." She looked ill, her face pale, her eyes watering.

"Let's get in the car."

She sat behind the wheel, her head bowed. It was the first time since I had met her in February that she had really lost her cool. "I don't know what's going on. I don't know why this is happening. I love that man. I want him to be alive, I want him to be in good health. I want him to love me as much as he loved me before Valentine's Day. Because I love him that much. There's nothing that could have happened that would change how I feel." Tears were flowing now, and she reached inside her purse for a tissue.

For the first time since we had met, I truly believed in the power of her love. I felt it as strongly as I felt my own love for Jack. I had no doubts about Jack's sincerity, about the depth of his feeling for me, and Carlotta felt the same way about Val. Whatever was going on, their relationship had not been changed—from her point of view.

"We'll find him," I said.

"Alive or dead?"

"I don't know yet. There are still a couple of possibilities, and I don't know which will turn out to be the right one."

"You mean Bambi."

"I wish you'd told me."

"It was over years ago. Jake knew about it because Jake knew everything. But what happened between them has no bearing on what happened on the lake."

I didn't want to say what I was thinking, that a gun aimed at Clark might have been responsible for a bullet in Matty if Matty tried to intervene, to save his friend. "Maybe it was over for Val, but not for Bambi," I said.

"It was over, Chris. Bambi and Clark were very happy together. I've never met two people who were more suited to each other."

"She had a funeral for her husband before his body turned up. You and Annie didn't."

"I didn't because I didn't believe Val was dead. I knew Matty and Clark were. They knew, too. And we were all right. Annie just wanted a body. And she got one." She looked at her watch. "Where do we go from here?"

"I want to call Jack. There's a directory called *Cole's* that all the detective squads in New York City have, where telephone numbers are listed first and names and addresses last, a sort of reverse listing. They provide a call-in service for out-of-town numbers, and I want to ask Jack to find out where this nine-oh-five number is. It may not tell us where the men were going that night, but it'll give us the name of the person who had that phone number, the address, the apartment, even some things about the area. There was no forwarding number, so I have no idea if he or she is still living there, with or without a new telephone, but I think we ought to go up there and knock on a door."

"But if the phone's disconnected, he's probably moved."

"Maybe the neighbors will know something. Whoever it is, that person had a relationship with Val. He may know things about Val that you and Jake don't know. Don't you think it's strange that a few months after the accident the phone is disconnected?"

"Very strange." She had started the car and was driving back the way we'd come. "Weird. Creepy."

"Maybe Val maintained a house in Canada."

"I would have seen the checks," Carlotta said quickly.

"But he made withdrawals all the time from his passbooks. He could have paid with a money order."

"But he called there, Chris. Who was he calling?"

"That's what we have to find out. I think Jack can help."

I called him when we got back to the house, but he wasn't at his desk. I knew I could ask Detective Murdock for the same favor, but I didn't want to involve him and didn't want to tell him any more than I had to. I left a message for Jack, thinking I would rather fly home and spend the weekend with him, but I decided to give it another couple of hours. When I got off the phone, Carlotta dialed the Ontario number herself, as if to confirm what I had told her. I watched her hang up after listening to the recorded message.

"I'd give anything to know when that phone was disconnected," she said.

"So would I."

"Why did your husband pick this day of all days to be away from his desk?"

"Sometimes duty calls."

"We're going to find him, Chris." She looked at the phone number she held in her hand. "I feel it. It's close now. We're really going to find him."

For the first time, I agreed with her. I just didn't know if we'd find him alive or dead.

Carlotta was really hyper now. She couldn't sit, couldn't read, couldn't even hold a conversation. I was aching to talk to Bambi again, but I didn't want to leave the phone in case Jack called. I wanted to be the one to ask him to look up the number in *Cole's*, not Carlotta. If he were out on a case, there was no telling when he would be back in the station house. A homicide could take eight hours of on-the-scene investigation, and there was no way I could contact him on the scene. She asked me once to try the number again, but I didn't want to bother him or the detective squad. I was pretty sure he would get my message; he would call back when he had the time.

At four, the phone finally rang. I picked it up.

"Hey, sorry it took so long," Jack's easygoing voice said. "How do you feel?"

"Fine. You out on a big case?"

"Big enough. Over four hours. We stopped to eat on the way back to the house. Man, were we empty. How's things?"

"I've made a discovery, and I need professional help."

"You psycho already? It usually takes about ten years on the job for most people."

"Professional doesn't always mean psychological," I said with a smile. "I need your *Cole's* connection."

"You got a number?"

"In Ontario, area code nine-oh-five. Val called the number every few days for years. Made the last call the morning of Valentine's Day. It's disconnected now."

"Sounds like a good lead. Give me the number and I'll get back to you."

I read it off and he promised to call back as soon as he had something.

"There should be a record of it," I said to Carlotta. "The directory is an annual one, so whatever was in it at the start of the year should be there now."

"And they'll have the name and address?"

"Even more than that," I said, repeating what Jack had told me some time ago. "They have information on the area, how populated it is, what the average income range is, things like that."

"I don't care about that. I just want to know who lives there."

"Or lived there," I said.

"Chris, what will we do if they're gone?"

"Talk to the neighbors. Try to trace a driver's license, or an auto license, if they drove a car. Let's not worry about those things right now."

But she was worried. I munched on some leftovers in her refrigerator and drank a glass of milk, but she couldn't eat. I knew that if Jack came up with an address, we would be out the door in seconds, and I felt better when my stomach had something in it. Finally, just about half an hour after I had spoken to Jack, the phone rang again.

Carlotta jumped up, but she let me answer.

"Got it," Jack said. "Got a pencil?"

"In my hand."

"OK. The subscriber is E. K. Winkel, and he lives at 27 Rosegarden Lane." He gave me the name of a town I had never heard of. "I looked it up," he said. "It's right on the Canadian side of Lake Erie, and the most prominent town that I can find in the area is something called Fort Erie. It's near the bridge between Buffalo and Ontario."

"Is there any indication of whether that's a man's name or a woman's?"

"None. I called Ontario information and asked for

E. K. Winkel, and they said there wasn't any listing for that name."

"So they may be gone."

"Gone or gave up a telephone."

"How can you live without a phone nowadays?"

"Makes it harder to find someone. If a guy's hiding out, information can't even say he has an unlisted number."

"Or they may have moved and left no forwarding number."

"Always a possibility."

"Well, I guess that's it."

"Sounds like I won't see you this weekend."

"I don't know at this point. I'll talk to Carlotta. If you don't hear from me, it's a no."

"Maybe I'll do some real cooking tomorrow, and the fumes will find their way to Buffalo."

"I'll breathe deeply," I said.

"Make sure the air is good."

We had a baby to worry about. It was nice.

We were out the door as fast as I had anticipated, stopping only for a map of Ontario that Carlotta put her hands on very quickly. Then we drove to Buffalo for the second time that day, this time entering at a different point and driving along the lake until we reached a bridge.

"I forgot to ask you," Carlotta said suddenly. "Do you have some ID on you?"

"My driver's license."

"That'll do. Are you American-born?"

"Definitely."

"No problem. Just tell the truth—if they ask you."

The Americans didn't much care who we were, but the Canadians asked a few questions. Carlotta said we'd be back after having dinner in Canada, and we scooted through. I looked at the map and directed her toward the town where the disconnected telephone had been.

"How often do you travel on your job?" I asked.

"Once every couple of weeks."

"Overnight?"

"Usually over one or two nights."

"Then Val could have driven to Canada while you were gone and visited someone on this side."

"I talked to him every night, Chris."

"Was he always home when you called?"

She was silent, her lips set. Finally she said, "Did you ever call your husband and find him not at home?"

"Many times."

"Well, it happened to me, too."

"Would you have any way of knowing whether he entered Canada?"

"No way I can think of. We keep books of bridge tickets in our cars, but I don't count his and he doesn't count mine. And he could have paid cash. He could as easily have driven to Rochester or Jamestown."

Neither of us said anything for a few minutes while I watched the road and the map alternately. Then Carlotta said, "The other direction is Niagara Falls. Maybe someday we'll be able to drive that way. It's a sight worth seeing."

"I'd like to see it."

"I'm very nervous."

"Would you like me to drive?"

She shook her head. I had the feeling she was sure we were about to knock on a door and find Val. I thought it was possible, but I wasn't as certain as she was.

"This is the town," I said as we passed a sign. "Slow

down. We're looking for Erie Street. That should take us to Rosegarden Lane."

She braked suddenly. "I can't do this."

"I'll drive," I said. I got out and walked around the car as Carlotta slid into the passenger seat. When I opened the car door, she was sitting with her head in her hands and her shoulders were shaking. "I can do this myself," I offered.

"No. I'm up to it. Thank God I didn't eat anything before we left the house. I'm sorry I'm falling apart. All the things I haven't wanted to think about are flooding my brain right now. And it's all hitting me right in the stomach."

"It'll all be over in a few minutes." I started down Erie, looking for the turn that would take me to the Winkel house.

"There it is," she said.

I turned left and we both looked at numbers.

"Keep going. We're in the sixties and the numbers are getting smaller."

Thirty-one was on the left side of the street. I parked across from it. "Let's give it a try. It's the next house."

We got out and crossed the street. The houses were all different, one a small frame with a front porch, one a larger brick with a double door. Number twenty-seven was smaller and made of wood, a single garage standing at the end of a narrow driveway. There were a few shrubs but no trees. Although the day had been mild, there was a stiff breeze, and I realized it must come in off the lake. Maybe trees didn't take to it, especially in winter.

"Let me go first," Carlotta said, as though she had recovered from her fright or thought it best to impress me with her newfound courage.

"Don't ask about Val," I warned. "We don't want to alert him that he's been found. He may decide to 'unfind' himself."

"OK." We went up the steps to the porch, and she pushed the bell. We could hear it clearly inside the house, but there was no other sound. Carlotta rang again. From somewhere inside a voice called something.

"Someone's there," Carlotta whispered. "It sounded like a girl."

"Let me do the talking."

"No. This is my husband. I'll handle it."

The door opened, and a sleepy girl about sixteen years old stood looking at us.

"I'm looking for Mr. or Ms. Winkel," Carlotta said. "Are they home?"

"No one's home except me."

"When do you expect them?"

The girl looked slightly dazed. "I don't know. Maybe tonight. Maybe after the weekend. What's this about? Who are you?" She looked from Carlotta to me.

"I'm Chris Bennett," I said, interrupting Carlotta before she could say her name or anything else that might compromise us. "Are you the Winkels' daughter?"

"Me? Gosh, no. I'm cat-sitting while they're away."

"I need to talk to them. You think they'll be home tonight?"

"I don't know when they'll be home."

"Maybe I could call them. Could you give me the telephone number?"

"They don't have a phone anymore, and I'm not allowed to give out that kind of information." She was looking more awake now and seemed to be sizing us up.

"Maybe you'd better come back next week. I don't think I can help you."

"Thank you very much," I said before Carlotta could prolong the conversation. The girl shut the door, snapping the lock audibly, and I took Carlotta's arm firmly and led her down the stairs.

"We could have asked—"

"No. That's it. Ask anything else and she'll tell a long story when these people get back, and maybe they'll run away again. She has my name, which is meaningless to them. I hope she's not good at remembering faces." I wanted to look back at the house to see if she was looking out the window, but I didn't dare.

"What now?"

"Now I think we get in the car and drive away and hope she hasn't looked at what we're driving."

"We can't leave, Chris. They may come back tonight. We have to be here when they do."

"Then we'll drive around the corner and park where she can't see us from the house and wait for a while. How's that?"

"That's good."

No one that I could see was watching us as we drove down the block and around the corner. We took three right turns and parked where someone coming from the center of town would have to pass us to reach the house.

Then she turned off the motor, and we waited.

21

We sat in silence, each of us with her own thoughts. Whatever Carlotta's were, I preferred not to know. My own were troublesome enough. I had let this case get completely out of hand, and I was to blame for the mess. I should never have allowed Carlotta to accompany me to this house. She had shown her face and could be described to whoever the residents of the house were. If this place were a kind of "safe house" for Val, he would recognize the description and might move on. I had gone too far in what I told Carlotta. I should have kept this address to myself, should have made some excuse to her and driven here alone.

It was too late now. It was also getting late in the evening, and my discomfort was growing. I didn't want to spend the night here, didn't want to spend one additional minute. I was hungry and uncomfortable, and with only one car between us, there was no way one of us could get into town while the other stood on the street, visible from every living room, and continued the vigil.

It was such a quiet and out-of-the-way area that almost no cars went by. We were sitting just close enough to the corner that we could see a piece of the Winkel house. Whoever the girl was, she used lights sparingly. One went on downstairs, and that was it. As far as I could see, no one went in or out of the front door.

Suddenly the light that was barely visible through the front windows went out, and I wondered if the girl was ready for bed at this early hour. A moment later the front door opened and she came out, turning toward the door to lock it. Then she bounced down the front steps, turned to her left, which was away from us, and started down the street.

Carlotta quickly opened the car door and got out, leaving the door ajar. She walked to the corner and looked down Rosegarden Lane. I could no longer see the girl from my seat.

Then Carlotta came back, got into the car, and closed the door. "She went to the end of the block and turned the corner. Maybe she's fed the cat, taken her nap, and she's gone home for the night."

"Sounds reasonable." I was starting to feel that I could not spend one more minute sitting in that car.

"I'm sorry. This is very cruel of me. If I'm hungry, you must be starving. The girl's gone, and we need a bathroom and a restaurant."

"That sounds good to me."

She started the motor and turned the headlights on. In a few minutes, we were in a pleasant, homey restaurant and I was stuffing bread into my mouth as though I hadn't eaten in ages.

"Here's what I think we should do," I said, when we had eaten enough that the pangs had been quieted. "You and I fly to New York tomorrow and you stay with me over the weekend."

"But—"

"I know. You want to come back here. The girl said they might not come back till after the weekend. Let's give them a couple of days. In the meantime, we'll go up to Connecticut and check out that cemetery. I want to see if a Matthew Franklin is buried there."

"You think that nurse's aide in Connecticut was running some sort of service for bringing children into the country?"

"It's possible. Maybe she came over, got herself trained, and took the job in the hospital. She could have access to their records at a time when few people were around. It's a strange way to make a living, but maybe she sold this information to people in eastern Europe who wanted to get their children to America."

"And then, when she couldn't find a dead child to suit a client, she killed one," Carlotta said.

"And left the country before they could arrest her."

"So who are the Winkels?"

"I have no idea. But they're obviously connected with Val. He phoned them regularly."

"Could they be blackmailing him?" she asked.

"I don't think so. If they were on bad terms, he would try to lose himself. He kept in touch with them. That has to mean there's some affection, some feeling."

"Chris, you don't think that girl is his child, do you?"

So that's what was bothering her. "I don't think so," I said, although I wasn't sure of anything at that point.

"If she's fifteen or sixteen, he could have been nineteen or twenty when—"

"Let's not speculate too much. Will you fly to New York with me tomorrow?"

"I want to come back here."

"We need two people and two cars so we can relieve

each other. The girl said they might come back tonight and might come back after the weekend. Let's give it till after the weekend."

She relented finally, and when we got back to her house, she made reservations for a flight the next day. I just hoped the girl at the Winkels' house had forgotten all about us after we left. Only one thing continued to trouble me: What if Val had been in the house all the time we were standing on the porch talking to the girl? If that had happened, we had lost him for good. And we might never find out about it.

Carlotta decided to spend the weekend with Amy Grant, whom she hadn't seen since February. I felt happy just to have a few hours on Saturday and Sunday in Jack's company and to eat his home-cooked food, which is the best I've ever had. The framing of the addition had moved along remarkably. There were solid walls of plywood now with neat rectangles where windows would be. I was fascinated with the progress and somewhat envious of the builders. They could see their accomplishment grow, board by board. In contrast, working on a case often seemed like a collection of so much litter until that lucky moment when the litter rearranged itself into the kind of structure that would yield a solution.

You're mixing metaphors, Kix, I told myself. But I really needed something to get that structure started. Was I any closer to finding Matty's killer? Was I closer to finding Val? I didn't know.

"So this girl told you there was no phone in the house anymore," Jack said, when we were talking about it.

"That's what she said. But I was wondering, could they have a cellular phone?"

"Sure, why not? Just carry it with you. Keep it in the car during the day and bring it home at night."

"Suppose they didn't want it identified with their home address?"

"Maybe they have a mailbox somewhere, or a business address to have it billed to."

"Then we have no way of finding that number. It might not even be in the name of Winkel."

"Could be a business name."

"It's amazing," I said, "how easy it is nowadays to lose yourself and still keep in touch. I rent a mailbox somewhere, call myself ABC Associates, and get a telephone that goes where I go. And you can't tie it to the Brooks family on Pine Brook Road."

"Lots of people do it."

On Sunday afternoon Carlotta and I drove to Connecticut. Jack, as usual, had plenty of studying to keep him busy. His finals were coming up and, assuming he did well, which I was sure he would, the end of his second year of evening law school, the halfway point. He promised another good meal when I got back, not that I needed an incentive. I drank another glass of skim milk and picked Carlotta up at Amy Grant's house.

"You're looking more relaxed," I said when we were on the way.

"Amy and I have a good time together. Most of our memories are happy ones."

"Have you booked a flight to Buffalo?"

"Two seats. You'll have to decide whether to come back with me tomorrow morning."

"I don't see how, Carlotta. I'm teaching Tuesday."

"We'll talk about it later. How's your morning sickness?"

"Still with me. But it only lasts about an hour. Then I feel pretty good."

"I hope this case comes to a satisfying end since it's going to be your last one."

"I hope so, too."

"Won't you miss doing this?"

"A little, maybe. I'll have plenty to keep me busy and happy."

We kept up the chatter till we were a few miles from the cemetery. Carlotta had the map open on her lap, and she guided me as though she had done it all before. Suddenly there was the iron fence that enclosed the grounds, the white stones beyond on the well cared-for grass. I turned into the lane between a pair of open gates.

At the main building we got out and went inside. A woman sat at a desk with a telephone and looked up as we approached.

"I'm looking for the grave of Valentine Krassky," I said without glancing at Carlotta.

She checked a book and wrote down the plot number and driving instructions on a pad, tearing the sheet off when she was done.

"And also Matthew Franklin," I said.

She opened the book again and looked through it. "I'm sorry, but there doesn't seem to be a grave for that name. Is it a recent burial?"

"No. It's quite a long time ago."

"Are you sure it's this cemetery?"

"Maybe I got it wrong," I said. "Thank you for the other one. We'll drive over."

"I'm not sure I want to see this," Carlotta said as I drove slowly on the winding road.

"You can stay in the car."

"Maybe Matty isn't part of the scam."

"Maybe the original was buried in another cemetery."

"Matty looks as American as any man I've ever known."

"We all come from somewhere, Carlotta."

"True."

"Here we are." I pulled to the side, leaving just enough room for one car to go by. We got out and walked, checking names as we went.

The stone was dark marble and read VALENTINE KRASSKY, with the dates of his birth and death, a mere six years apart.

Carlotta began to cry. "How could anyone kill a child?" she said.

In front of the stone was a fresh bouquet of flowers. "His parents must have come here," I said. "I'm afraid I stirred up the misery in their lives."

Carlotta turned away and started walking. I let her go. We had made this long trip and learned nothing. Matty's namesake wasn't buried here, if indeed there were one. I couldn't go around to all the cemeteries in Connecticut, and there was no guarantee that the namesake was even from Connecticut. The mysterious woman with the accent might have worked in another state before or after working around here.

I looked around for Carlotta but didn't see her. She wasn't in the car, and she didn't seem to be in the direction she had wandered off in. I started walking myself, looking idly at the stones as though Matty's name might materialize on one of them, but, of course, it didn't.

Ahead of me a group was gathered, and I realized a funeral was taking place.

It took me a minute to recognize the sound of my own name being called from far away. I stopped and turned around, shading my eyes from the bright sun. Carlotta was waving through the trees, signaling me to come to her. I was wearing my sneakers so I ran, not very fast, but I got there quickly.

"Look at this," Carlotta said, pointing.

I stood in front of a simple stone that read CLARK ANDREW THAYER, BELOVED SON, AGE TWO, and the dates of the child's birth and death. A terrible chill went through me. All three men were linked in life and in death, maybe in two deaths apiece.

"What do we do now?" Carlotta asked.

I ignored the question. "Was Clark younger than Val and Matty? It looks like it from the date of his birth."

"He said he was."

"This boy died before Val Krassky. Maybe Val was the last of the lot, and she was in a hurry to get it done."

"You think she killed this one, too?"

"I have no way of knowing, and I don't want to upset another family. One was too much. Let's drive back." The beginnings of a theory were finally starting to form. Something Bambi had said to me. Maybe she had gotten it wrong. Maybe . . . "Stay over till Tuesday. I'll fly back with you Tuesday afternoon, after I've taught my class. Maybe we can put all this to rest—with a little luck."

"What are you thinking?"

We walked toward the car. "I think there was a blood relationship. I think they seemed as close as brothers because they were brothers."

"Is that why Val kept that life insurance policy?

Because Matty was his brother, and he wasn't doing well and Val wanted to look after him?"

"Maybe," I said. "And maybe it was more than that. But I think we have a good chance of finding out now."

"Do you think Val's alive?"

"I still can't tell you that. But if he's alive, I think the Winkels know. And we may be able to persuade them to tell us. Now that we're armed with information."

"You don't think Tuesday's too late?"

"I think they'll come back to that house," I said. "We'll talk to them. Right on Rosegarden Lane."

22

I knew that Monday was a hard day for Carlotta, but it was a very pleasant day for me. I got to walk with Melanie early in the morning, got to watch the builders as they worked on the addition, got to see my husband when he came home late in the evening after his class. Of such simple things is pleasure made.

When I had a minute I called information in Ontario for a number for Winkel at the Rosegarden Lane address, but there was none, not even an unlisted one. I asked for a number in the name of Krassky but that, too, yielded nothing.

I had little preparation for my class; tomorrow was the last one of the semester. Next Tuesday I would give my final, and all that remained was a thorough review of the poems and poets we had covered. It was the sort of thing I could do with my eyes closed.

The class went well, but several students lingered when it was over, trying to get me to disclose the exact questions that would be on the final. It never failed, and I never failed to keep it all to myself. When the last of them gave up, I dashed to my car and drove home, picked up my suitcase, called Jack to say good-bye, and went to Amy Grant's house to get Carlotta. She came out wearing pants and a blouse with a kind of jacket-shirt over all, as the day was cool and breezy. She put her bag in the backseat, and we started for La Guardia.

"That's a beautiful shirt," I said. "It's just right on a day like this."

"It's Val's. He got it last year and I've worn it more than he ever did." She rubbed a sleeve, feeling the fineness of the fabric.

I started to say something, but my mind did a little jig, and those pieces of litter that were really unconnected scraps of information started to move toward that elusive structure.

"Did you say something?" Carlotta asked.

"No. Sorry, I was just thinking."

She laughed. "You don't have to apologize for that. It's neither immoral nor fattening."

But this time it had been productive. Finally.

I persuaded Carlotta to stay home, and I took Val's Mercedes and drove to Bambi Thayer's house. A little girl who looked very much like Bambi was standing on the driveway talking to another little girl. I parked at the curb and walked over to the children. "Are you Mrs. Thayer's daughter?" I asked the obvious look-alike.

"Uh-huh."

"Is she home?"

"She's in the back. Who are you?"

"Chris Bennett."

"Oh."

"I was sorry to hear about your daddy," I said.

She said, "Thank you," as though she had been told how to respond.

"I didn't know him but I heard he was a wonderful person."

"He was."

"I'm sure you'll always remember him. When was the last time you saw him?"

"He came home from the store before he went out to dinner with Uncle Val and Uncle Matty. It was Uncle Val's birthday."

"Yes, I remember. Can I go in the back and find your mom?"

"Sure."

I walked along a path at the side of the house and came to a splendid backyard. Bambi was sitting on a deck watching a small television set. I called, "Hi."

"Oh. It's you." She leaned over and shut off the TV. "Come on up."

I went up and sat in the second chair. "It's beautiful back here."

"I love it. Clark and I used to sit here all the time."

"Bambi, is it possible that Clark went to some other high school besides Bennett?"

"Why do you ask?"

"Because Bennett has no record of his being a student there."

She looked confused. "Why would you even ask them?"

"Because I've learned some funny things about Val and Matty. It seems they lived in the same house during high school."

"Maybe that's how they got to be friends."

"Maybe." I didn't want to tell her any more than I had to. "But Clark doesn't seem to have gone to Bennett."

"Well, he said he did. They probably just lost the

records. It's a stupid thing to lie about. If he said he went there, he went there."

"Did he ever mention a family named Winkel?"

"I don't think so."

"You dated Val at one time, didn't you?"

Her look turned to disgust. "Please go away," she said. "My husband is dead. All our husbands are dead. Where is this taking you? Why do you have to dredge up the past? It's gone. Can't you let it be gone?" She looked away, composing herself. "It doesn't mean anything. Didn't you ever have a boyfriend before you got married?"

It was one of those moments when I saw myself as different. "I didn't," I said. "I was a nun for almost fifteen years."

"A nun." Her eyebrows went up and her face softened. "I didn't know. I'm sorry. I didn't mean to say anything that would offend you."

"You didn't. I left the convent when I was thirty and met my husband soon after. We were married about a year later. I'm afraid dating is something I never did in my life."

"That's weird." Of the three wives, she seemed the youngest, the sweetest, and the most innocent. Now she seemed a little nonplussed.

"Will you tell me about you and Val?"

"It was nothing. I met him at a party and we went out for a while. He was in college, and I went out there to visit him. That's how I met Jake. Jake told you about it, didn't he?"

"Yes."

"I think he had the feeling it was hot and heavy, and maybe it was, but Val wasn't for me and I sure wasn't for

Val. A couple of years later, Val told Clark to give me a call. It didn't work out right away but when it did, it was right."

"That was nice of Val."

"He was a nice guy. They were all nice guys." Her eyes filled.

"Did Clark know you had gone out with Val?"

She pressed her lips together. "He knew Val knew me. Clark was a very old-fashioned kind of man. It might have upset him if he'd known I'd had a—relationship with his friend."

"So you don't think Clark ever found out that it was more than a date or two?"

"He didn't hear it from me. Carlotta wasn't around when it happened, and neither was Annie."

"But Jake was," I said.

"Why would Jake say anything?"

"Did Jake ever hang out with the three men?"

"Sometimes."

"Bambi, you told me last time we talked that Annie came from New York City or New Jersey. Are you sure of that?"

"Somewhere around there," she said. "One place is as good as another. She's not from around here."

I stood and thanked her for talking to me. Then I went down the stairs to the lawn and around the house to the street. The little girls were gone, but a few toys had been left carelessly on the driveway. I picked them up and put them on the edge of the grass.

So much came back to Jake. Jake knew about the mysterious phone calls to Canada. Jake knew about the brief but torrid relationship Val had had with Bambi. Jake knew that Val had known Annie before she met Matty.

But Jake hadn't given up anything willingly. I had had to pry information out of him, make far-fetched guesses that he then confirmed. If he knew things that Val wanted kept secret, he had certainly appeared to be trying to keep them from me.

I worked my way over to Annie Franklin's house. Here, too, children were playing in the street and on driveways. I thought of the little being that was growing inside me. Would I ever be relaxed enough as a mother to let my child play on Pine Brook Road? Would I be able to let my child out of my sight? At this time, they were unanswerable questions.

I parked a couple of houses away from Annie's and walked to her driveway where some boys were shooting baskets. I tried to pick out the one who was Matty and Annie's son, but this time I failed. As I stood watching, a boy about eight or nine grabbed the ball and turned to me.

"You lookin' for my mom?"

"Yes. Is she inside?"

"Yeah, I think so."

"I'm Chris Bennett. What's your name?"

"Matt."

"Hi, Matt. I'm sorry about your dad."

"Yeah." He looked pained.

"I didn't know him but I heard he was a very nice person."

"Yeah, he was."

"When did you see him for the last time?"

"The night it happened. I was in bed already, and he came home to put his other boots on. He came in my room and said good night."

I tried to keep my excitement to myself. *Matty had come home that night.* "It's nice that you saw him."

"Yeah. I remember it. You wanna go inside and look for my mom?"

"Yes."

"Go in the front door. It's open." He turned to his pals and tossed the ball.

I didn't want to let on that I knew. Annie had lied to me. If her son had seen Matty, she had seen him, too. I rang the doorbell, putting it together. Matty had owned a handgun, whether Annie knew about it or not, and he had picked it up when he went home to change his boots. Somehow, as he held the gun on one of the other two men on the ice, one of them had managed to turn it back on Matty.

It had to be Val, I thought. From everyone's description of Clark, he didn't seem like the one to shoot at his oldest friend.

"Hi, Chris. Come in." Annie had opened the door.

"It's lovely out this evening."

"Yes. I should be out there instead of in here." She was wearing black jeans and a shirt of faded blue. She took me through the house to the room at the back. "Sit anywhere. I can't believe you still have questions."

My big question had now been answered, and I had to be careful how I phrased the smaller questions so she wouldn't guess that I knew about Matty coming home. "I've been thinking about Matty's mother," I said, coming in from left field. "I think you said she lived in England."

"That's what he told me."

"Did you look for an address for her after the accident?"

"I wouldn't know where to look. I keep the family address book."

"Maybe he kept it at work."

"Why would he do that? And why do you care? I don't see what difference this makes."

"I'm looking for anything that will explain who killed Matty and why. And if Val is still alive, I want to find him."

"If he didn't drown, he probably left the country after he killed Matty."

"His passport's in his drawer."

That seemed to surprise her. "So what, if Matty didn't keep his mother's address?"

"Val didn't keep his mother's, either."

She frowned. "So that's what they had in common. They hated their mothers. What else is new?"

"I wondered if you had any pictures I could look at," I said. "The three men and the three wives. I'd like to see them."

"Tons of them. I look at them every night now." She got up and went to a drawer in a built-in cabinet, pulled out a couple of thick albums, and brought them over. "How far back do you want to go?"

"Just the last year." It was something Joseph had said.

"Start at the end of this one and go backwards."

"Thanks, Annie." I opened it at the end, where there were several blank pages, and flipped back to the last pictures ever taken of the three families before they were destroyed. In the very first group, I saw something that jolted me, but I kept my eyes on the page and then turned back to the preceding one.

"Where were these taken?" I asked conversationally, although I didn't care.

"We went on a skiing weekend in January. It was the last time we were all there together."

"You all look very happy."

"We were." She sat across from me.

"No kids?" I asked.

"We left them home. It was a grown-up weekend."

I turned another page and there was Christmas morning. The tree was tall and beautifully decorated. Annie was there in an elegant negligee, the children in pajamas, Matty already dressed in a plaid shirt as though he were about to go hunting in the winter woods.

"Anything special you're looking for?" Annie asked.

"I just wanted to see what everyone looked like. And everyone looked so happy."

"We were happy."

"Are you going to stay here, Annie?"

"In the house? Sure. My kids go to school here. The house is paid for."

"That's wonderful."

"Matty had mortgage insurance. It was expensive, but it was worth it. I have the house free and clear now. All I pay is the taxes."

But she would never have the million dollars of insurance to add to her bank account. Did she know about it? It had become a crucial question, and I couldn't ask her. She would never admit it if she did, so whatever she answered would be irrelevant.

I turned another few pages and then closed the book. "This is really heart-wrenching," I said. "Three beautiful families."

She nodded, her eyes filling as Bambi's had. These were two wounded women, and their pain was real, as was their children's.

"Where did you come from before you married Matty?" I asked, finally getting to what I needed to know.

"Greenwich."

"Connecticut?"

"Yes. My father is a lawyer there. I grew up there."

"I've heard it's a lovely town." I could feel my heart pounding.

"It is."

"Thank you for showing me the pictures, Annie."

"Have you figured anything out yet?"

"A few things. I'll let you know when it all comes together."

Carlotta was waiting for me, watching out the window as I drove up the driveway.

"Anything new?" she asked.

"A couple of things. Can we have dinner and then drive to Canada? I think we may be able to settle things tonight."

"Are you serious? What have you learned?"

"I think I know what happened on the ice. I even think I know why. The Winkels can fill in the holes in the story."

She stared at me. "Aren't you going to tell me?"

"I'll tell you in Canada. Sister Joseph was right. The red scarf was the key. Let's go. I'm starving."

23

You didn't have to be particularly astute to sense that Carlotta was angry with me. She wanted to know everything that I knew, but now I knew better than to tell her. So much depended on how the Winkels reacted when we confronted them. I would have preferred to see them alone, but that was out of the question. Carlotta was not about to let me out of her sight.

It was dark when we got to Canada—Carlotta explained at the border that we were visiting relatives, which wasn't so far from the truth—but we found the house on Rosegarden Lane with no difficulty. We parked around the corner where the car couldn't be seen and walked to the little house, which was alive with light, upstairs and downstairs. I rang the doorbell and I stood in front of the door, Carlotta at my side.

The door opened almost immediately, and a grandmotherly-looking woman with steel-gray hair pulled back in a bun and steel-rimmed glasses on her lined face stood before us. "Yes?"

"Mrs. Winkel, my name is Christine Bennett. I want to talk to you about the three men who were in the accident on the lake on Valentine's Day."

"Why should I know about that?" she said, and now

that she spoke a whole sentence, her German accent was obvious.

"Because those three men who fell through the ice were your grandsons." I hadn't been sure till I saw her, but she was in her late seventies at least, too old to be the mother of a thirty-five-year-old.

"You have the wrong house," she said, trying to shut the door.

"I have the right house. Please let us come in and talk to you."

"There is nothing to say."

"I know what happened in the hospital in Connecticut thirty years ago."

That got to her. She opened the door all the way and we walked in. The living room was furnished in a comfortable, old-fashioned style: chairs you could sink into, an Oriental rug that was worn but still attractive. I found the one hard chair in the room and took it for myself.

"You talk. When you're finished, maybe I say something, maybe I don't."

There were a lot of holes in what I knew, and I wanted to impress her with what I knew, not with what was missing, so I chose my words carefully, neglecting details when I wasn't certain of them. "You brought three grandsons into Canada when they were young. Your daughter went to Connecticut and became a nurse's aide. She worked in a hospital where she had access to the records of children who had died. She used their names to get American birth certificates for your grandsons."

The woman kept her face as immobile as a block of granite, but her eyes reflected the anguish she was feeling, and the surprise. I had no doubt that this was the first time anyone had presented her with this set of facts.

"There is evidence," I said, "that she killed the last of the three boys to hurry along the process."

"Is this what you came here to tell me?"

"I came here to find out if Val is still alive. His body has not been found."

"I don't know what you're talking about."

But she did know, and I had to get it out of her. "Is Mr. Winkel at home?"

"Mr. Winkel died three years ago."

So there was a Mr. Winkel. And maybe that could explain something that had confused me. "Did Clark live with Mr. Winkel?" I asked. "I know that you and the other two boys lived in Stanley Kazmarek's house in Buffalo, over near Starin."

"Where do you get these things? Where do you get this nonsense from?"

"Bennett High School had the address, and then I met Mr. Kazmarek and he told me. And I talked to a neighbor's son who was friends with Matty. Did you call the boys Matty and Val or did you call them by their birth names?"

"Get out of my house."

"I can't go. I have to know about Val."

"Why? Are you his wife?"

"I'm his wife." Carlotta stood and faced the old woman. "And I love him. I don't care if his mother was a killer. He's my husband, and I want to spend the rest of my life with him."

I think I suspected that he was alive and in the house when we walked down the street and I saw all the lights on. I became more certain when I saw the old, worn furniture and heard that Mr. Winkel was not alive. Like the nuns at St. Stephen's who counted every penny, this was not a woman who would leave lights on if she weren't in a room. The girl who had been cat-sitting had left the house dark when she locked the door. If lights were on upstairs, someone was there.

I turned to Carlotta. "I think he's upstairs."

"Val? You think Val's up there?"

"I do."

She lost her color, and for a moment I thought she might faint. But she steadied herself on a chair, then turned and looked for the stairs, which were against the left wall. She walked over and stood looking up. "Val?" she called shakily. "Val, it's me, Carlotta." There wasn't a sound. "Please come down and talk to me. I love you. I don't care what happened on the ice. I don't care who killed Matty. I don't care if your mother killed someone. I'm your wife, and I can't live without you." There were tears on her cheeks, and my own eyes were misting over.

I was standing beside her now, and she looked at me as though I could make it happen, make him be alive, make him come down the stairs. I touched her shoulder and nodded.

"Please, Val," she called. "Whatever has to be done, we can do it together. You have to come down."

There was a sound then, the squeak of a spring, a heavy footstep. My heart was beating as fast as I was sure Carlotta's was. She gasped as whoever it was began to descend the stairs.

When Val reached the bottom step, he and his wife wrapped their arms around each other, crying. I turned away, my own tears spilling over. In the little living room, Mrs. Winkel had stood and was looking out the window, her back to the emotional scene at the foot of the stairs. All the secrets she had kept so diligently for so many years were out in the open now. I wondered how she would handle it.

I went over and stood beside her. "It's for the best," I said.

"No," she said, "it's all over. Where are my boys? Where are my beautiful boys? Dead in that cold lake, and I am dead with them."

24

"I killed Matty," the big, bearded man at the kitchen table said. The beard was new and vaguely red, hinting at a deep rusty color. He looked thinner than in his pictures and older than thirty-five. But there was no doubt that seeing his wife had revived his spirits. He held her to him, looked at her face again and again as though to renew its image in his mind. "It was an accident, but I did it."

"Whose gun was it?" I asked. We had all been introduced, and the grandmother had made coffee and cut a cake but would not join us at the table.

"Matty's. He stopped at home after we had dinner at Giordano's. He must have picked it up then."

"Who was he going to shoot?" Carlotta asked.

Val shook his head. "It's complicated. There's a lot I never told you. I got the gun away from him and it went off. The ice was thin and he went down. Clark tried to help, but he went in, too."

"Where's the gun now?" I asked.

"I got rid of it."

"When did you leave your watch in the car?" I asked.

"After the accident. I wanted people to think I'd gone down with the other two. The back of the car was open. I climbed in just far enough to drop it on the backseat.

Then I got a bus to Buffalo and changed for a bus to Canada. I've been here ever since."

"If only you had let me know," Carlotta said.

"I couldn't. They might have checked the phone for incoming and outgoing calls. I didn't want to get you in trouble."

"Did you call Jake?" I asked.

He gave me a long, sad look. "I called him, but I didn't say anything. I hoped he would understand. I don't know if he did."

"I don't know either. He never said anything."

"How did you trace me here?"

"I found this number on last year's phone bills. Jake stalled for a while—he didn't want me to see them—but eventually he gave them to me. My husband's an NYPD detective and he was able to get the location."

"But we disconnected the phone on February fifteenth."

"It's still listed in this year's *Cole's* directory. Once a record of information has been made, it doesn't just disappear."

He shook his head. "It's not so easy to lose yourself."

It was the opposite of what I had said to Jack over the weekend. "Val, I'd like to hear the story, the whole story."

"I told you. I killed Matty by accident. There isn't anything else."

"Were Matty and Clark your brothers?"

"So you know that, too. They were my cousins. They were brothers."

"When did you come to Canada for the first time?"

"When I was a kid. I'm not sure of the year. We'd

been learning English for a long time. I have very vague memories of the sea voyage. My clearest recollections begin in Canada, and then in the States when we moved."

It didn't sound unreasonable. "How did your family tell you about your new name?"

"It was like a game at first. Then they explained it was very serious, that I was really Val Krassky, that my original name had been the game. When I got older, they told me the truth, but by then there wasn't much I could do about it. I understood that we had had to leave East Germany for our own good, that everyone in my family had made tremendous sacrifices so that we could come here. I knew I was named for someone who was about my age and who had died, and that the same was true of my cousins. No one except for the three of us, our grandparents, and my mother knew the real truth. We made up stories to tell our wives, but that's all they were, stories."

"Jake said you seemed to fall off the world when you left school for holidays."

"I did. I went to Canada to visit my grandparents. Jake never had a phone number for me or an address until I was on my own."

"Val," I said, "you're leaving out a lot that you know. I'm sure you know why that gun was on the ice in February."

"I told you; it's complicated. And it doesn't matter. I ended up causing the death of my closest friends, who happened to be my cousins."

"Did it have something to do with the insurance policy Carlotta found in your safe deposit box?"

"It was a personal thing," he said. "That's all I can say."

"Tell me about the three bankbooks in your desk drawer."

"One was for Carlotta, one was for Clark, and one was for my grandmother. It's all designated in my will."

"And the insurance policy was for Matty."

"Right."

"That's ten times as much as you were leaving to the others."

"Matty needed it."

"But why, Val?" Carlotta said. "A million dollars is a lot of money."

"He's dead. I can't discuss his problems."

"The bankbooks had a lot of withdrawals," I said. "You weren't just saving money. You were spending it."

"I was sending it to my grandmother. I'm her main means of support. She has a small pension. I wanted her to live well."

"There are some strange things about the shooting," I said. "There was a red scarf lying on the ice when the police helicopter went over the spot the next day."

"I don't know anything about a red scarf."

"It's the scarf you and Carlotta gave Matty for Christmas. If you shot him, why didn't it go down with him? Why didn't it have blood on it?" I was desperate to break his story, to get him to tell me the truth.

"I don't know what you're talking about. It must have fallen on the ice. I just don't remember. And it was dark."

"I wish you would tell us the truth," I said.

"I will tell you the truth," the strong voice of Grandmother Winkel declared. "This boy, he never shot anyone. I know him his whole life. Matty? Maybe he could shoot someone, but not this one. This is a good boy. You want to know what happened from the beginning? I tell you the story." She pulled a kitchen chair out and sat heavily. Then she began speaking.

25

"In the beginning we lived in the east, what was called the German Democratic Republic. I had two daughters and a son. My son was a sailor on a merchant ship. He never married. My daughters married. One had two sons, the other had one. The first daughter, Beate, she died when her sons were young. The second daughter, Petra, she took her sister's boys and raised them like her own. I helped. Petra was a nurse in Germany. It was a hard life, and we wanted to get out. We wanted the boys to have a good life. In those days you could pay the ship's master, and he would take you on board and get you to Canada. My son arranged it. My daughter went as a cook, and the boys dressed like little sailors. My husband and I, we also worked on the ship. The trip cost us everything we had in the world.

"We got into Canada, and first we lived in one place and then we lived in another. But what we wanted for the boys was to be citizens of the United States, and we had no papers. But we heard you could get them if you used the name of a dead person, and my daughter decided she would try to find three good names across the border.

"She left the boys with us and went to the States. She was a nurse in Germany, so it was easy to become a

238

nurse's aid in the U.S. She thought she would get a job, she would earn a living, she would bring us all over. Somebody told her, you go to a cemetery, you walk around, you find a dead person the right age and you get his papers. But she didn't have to do that. She got herself a job in a hospital in Connecticut, and then she could look at the records. She worked at night when it was quiet. She said she was going for lunch, but really she was looking at the records."

I noticed that Carlotta's eyes were fixed on the old woman, but Val hardly looked at her. His arm was around his wife, but his eyes were everywhere except on his grandmother.

"First she found Clark, the little one," Mrs. Winkel continued. "She went to the town hall, she filled out the papers, and they sent her the birth certificate, as if she was the little boy's mother. What did they know? She had the mother's name, she had the boy's name, she had the boy's birthday. It was like a miracle. Suddenly her little nephew was an American citizen. Then she found a record for Matty. It was a baby who died a day after he was born. It was a different town, so nobody there knew her. In a little while, she had another birth certificate." She paused, knowing she was coming to the most painful episode of all.

"And then there was Val," she said. "In the files she couldn't find a boy the right age. She looked and looked but there was nothing. But one night when she came to the hospital, there was a sick boy just as old as Val. He was very sick, he couldn't breathe, he needed—" She stopped and turned to Val. *"Was ist Sauerstoff?"*

"Oxygen," he said without looking at her.

"He needed oxygen. His lungs were no good. My

daughter looked at the medical record when she went into his room. This boy, he had been in the hospital before, always the same thing." She patted her chest.

I found myself tensing in anticipation of what I knew was coming, almost hoping the story would change and the little boy in the hospital bed would survive.

"That night," Mrs. Winkel said, "the boy died. The next morning, my daughter came back to Canada. I wrote for the birth certificate later, and we had it sent to an address in Buffalo."

"Where was your daughter?" I asked, although I knew.

"She went back to Germany."

"Why is that?"

"There was some funny business in the hospital. It was better she should go back."

"What was the funny business?" I asked. I was sure now that the grandmother knew something about the death of the child in the hospital.

"It was nothing, really. She wanted to live in Germany."

"Without her son?"

"It was better that way. He was safe with me."

"In that hospital," I said, "they think your daughter killed that little boy."

"My daughter was a nurse. She didn't kill anyone. When the boy was dead, she wrote down his name and address. That's all."

I could sense the strength of this woman. Her face had showed no emotion as she spoke, as she related this tale of adventure and crime. She was a woman who could handle adversity, who could take on the raising of three young boys whose parents were not there. It was just another thing she had to do, and she would do it well.

With her strength came power. The boys were devoted to her. In his worst moment, Val had gone to her, and she had taken him in and protected him.

"Many people connected with that hospital think the boy was killed. He was getting better the night he died. The last person in his room was your daughter. People saw her there."

"You are telling me my daughter is a killer? What do you know of killing? What do you know of the kind of life we lived over there? Have you ever lived in fear?" Her eyes pierced mine. "We had to get these boys away from that. We had to give them a good life. If a weak boy died, a strong one lived."

The audible gasp came from Carlotta, although it could have been mine. We had just heard a justification for the murder of an innocent child. Val mumbled something in German to his grandmother.

"When did the boys come to the States?" I asked, suppressing my urge to argue the point. "In high school?"

"Maybe a little before."

"But they lived in different places, didn't they?"

"My husband took the youngest. The two oldest ones came with me. They were too much for my husband. And we didn't want three boys with three different last names living in the same house. Maybe people would ask questions."

"So Clark lied about going to Bennett," I said.

"Clark lied," Val said. "Who would check something like that? Bambi?"

"What happened on weekends, Mrs. Winkel?"

"We went to Canada. Maybe we would visit my husband in his house."

"When did you buy this house?"

"My grandson bought it for us when he started to make some money. My grandson is a good boy." It was clear which grandson she was talking about.

"And he called you every week, every few days."

"Something is wrong with that?"

"I was just asking." She was the embodiment of the legendary feared sadistic nun who was said to rule every convent school, but I had never met the likes of this one. "What did you do when the boys finished high school?"

"We came back to Canada. We felt safer here. We never got our papers over there. I don't like to cross the bridge anymore. It makes me nervous."

I was rather glad something did. "Can you tell me what happened on the ice last February?"

She shrugged. "It was an accident. The boys thought it would be good fun to come over and visit their grandma. There was an accident, and two of them died."

"One of them was shot," I reminded her.

"It was an accident. Two of my boys are gone. But there are great-grandchildren now. Maybe I get to see them one day."

I turned to Val. "It wasn't as simple as that, was it? You know that the accident was that the wrong man was killed."

"What do you mean?" Carlotta said. "Who was supposed to get killed out there?"

I waited for Val to say it. Just as I thought he would not answer, he said softly, "I was."

"Don't say anything more," his grandmother cautioned. "We've said enough."

"It's too late to keep secrets, Mrs. Winkel," I said. "I know what happened that night."

"You can't know," Carlotta said. "How can you possibly know?"

"Because of the red scarf. The red scarf was lying on the ice."

"So what? It was Matty's. Why shouldn't it have been lying on the ice?"

"Because Matty wasn't wearing it," I said.

They all looked at me, and Val said, "She's right. Matty wasn't wearing it. If he'd been wearing it, it would've gone down with him."

"Val, what happened?" Carlotta asked.

He took his arm from around her and clapped his hands together quietly. Then he looked down at his hands for a moment before speaking. "Annie was wearing the scarf."

"Annie! What was she doing on the ice?"

"She came to kill me. That's what she was doing."

"How did she know—?"

"We stopped at the house so Matty could change his shoes. He told her what we were doing. After we left, she followed us with the other car."

"But the children," Carlotta said.

"She must have figured they were asleep."

At least one of them hadn't been, the boy who told me his father had come in to say good night to him. "When did you know she was following you?" I asked.

"Not for hours. We were most of the way across the lake. Matty was leading, I was bringing up the rear. All of a sudden there was a shot, and something skittered along the ice next to my leg. We turned around and flashed the light over the ice."

"You had a flashlight with you?"

"Matty had picked it up when he went home. It was a

good one, very bright with a wide sweep. He turned it toward the direction we'd come from, and there she was. Matty said, 'Shit, I think it's Annie,' and we turned back to find her. He thought something had happened at home, maybe the kids. So back we went. And when we got to where we could see her clearly, we saw the gun in her hand."

"My God," Carlotta said.

"That's how I felt. I knew who the gun was meant for."

"But why?"

"Because she knew I was a ghost. She came from Connecticut, not where my mother had worked but close enough, and she was a cousin of the Krassky family. She knew about the kid who died in the hospital, and when she came to Buffalo for a job, she met me and she put everything together."

"Was she blackmailing you?" I asked.

"Yeah, but not very actively. I gave her money from time to time, but not a lot. She wanted a big lump sum, and I said I couldn't do it. So we agreed I'd take out a life insurance policy with Matty as the beneficiary. This was around the time they were getting married. I gave her proof of the policy and proof that I kept the premiums paid. But then Matty lost his job last year, and she wanted a big sum to get him started on something new."

"I assume the threat was that she'd tell what she knew about your mother."

"Exactly. Her father's a hotshot lawyer. She threatened an international search for my mother. And that would embarrass me, and through me, Carlotta. She would also blow my cover and possibly get me in trouble with Immigration. She was holding all these things over my head and becoming more and more demanding. I didn't want Carlotta to know, and the longer I kept it from her, the less I wanted her to find out. I should have told you," he said, looking at her.

"So she decided to kill you to inherit the million dollars," I said.

"That must have been her plan. She must have been following us, and thought she could get off one shot and then turn back while the guys were looking after me. But she missed, and then she started to go nuts. She ranted about a relationship between us. It was crazy, but I figured it was for Clark's benefit, maybe for Matty's, too. She would shoot me because I'd done something terrible to her. Therefore I deserved to die."

"What happened?" I asked.

"We all saw it coming. There was nowhere to go, nowhere to hide. Matty started moving towards her and Clark did, too, but she kept that gun right on me. I zigged and zagged a little, and then, just as I sensed she was about to shoot, Matty lunged at her, grabbing for the gun. When it went off, it hit him instead of me."

"How terrible."

"He got a handful of the scarf. I can still see it flying. The force of the bullet threw him way back, and when he went down on the ice, it cracked and he dropped into the water. But the scarf fell near Annie and ended up on the ice."

"And the gun?"

"I'm not sure, but I think it may have gone down with Matty."

"How did Clark drown?"

"He was right near where Matty hit the ice. I think he was just drawn into the water with Matty."

"Which left you and Annie on the ice together."

"On dangerously thin ice. It was dark. The flashlight was gone. Matty had tried to use it to deflect the gun, and I don't know what happened to it. Matty and Clark were gone. I called, but there wasn't even a splash after they went down. Annie screamed Matty's name once, and then she just whimpered a lot. Then she was gone. It was snowing by then. I knew it was hopeless to try to find Matty and Clark. I'd end up dead, too. So I turned and went back, trying to follow our trail before it got snowed over. I didn't know if Annie still had the gun, so I had to be careful to stay out of her way. She must have been ahead of me the whole time, because I never caught up with her. By the time I got back to the beach, it was really snowing. I could see Annie's car parked next to Matty's, but I took a long detour so it wouldn't look as if I'd had anything to do with Matty's car. And then I thought I'd like to be considered dead to give me some time to think. So I circled back to the car—Annie was gone by then—and tried all the doors. The hatchback was open, and I climbed in and dropped my watch in the backseat as if I'd left it there to keep it safe while we crossed the lake. Then I backed out and found a bus to Buffalo. I think you know the rest."

I did. Most of it. "Did you talk to Annie?"

"I called her from here before I had the phone disconnected. She answered, but I didn't say anything. She sounded pretty agitated, so I hung on till she hung up. I never said a word, but I sensed she knew who was calling. I wanted her to know I was still out there, even if she had her story put together for that night."

"Val," I said, "something is troubling me. You said Annie knew you were a 'ghost.' But Matty and Clark were 'ghosts,' too. How could she disclose what she knew about you without the same thing coming out about her very own husband?"

"She didn't know about her very own husband. She didn't know about Clark. All she knew about was me."

"You never told her about the other two?"

"Why should I? It was their secret as much as mine was my secret. I'm not a blackmailer. And now that the Wall is down in Germany, my mother's probably pretty easy to find if anyone wants to put a little effort into it."

I found I was filled with admiration for this man. What had happened had been imposed upon him by a ruthless mother and backed up by a ruthless grandmother. He had tried to live with fictions and restrictions his family had saddled him with, and yet he remained honorable, loyal, and loving to his cousins and to the grandmother who was the architect of his shadowy life.

"When did you learn about your identity?" I asked.

"We knew about it as we grew up. We never used our real names, even when we were alone. We only spoke English. We knew we were different, but we learned how to be real Americans and blend in."

"When did you find out about what happened in the hospital in Connecticut?"

His eyes flicked over to his grandmother. "I was in my twenties. I was single. Annie walked into my life and hit me with the story. I knew I hadn't been born Valentine Krassky, that it was the name of someone my age who had died as a child. Suddenly she seemed to know more about it than I did. I didn't know what to say. I knew the birth certificate I used came from Connecticut, but I never imagined there was a scandal attached to it. I drove across the border and asked my grandparents."

"And that was the first you knew?" Carlotta said.

"That was it. My grandmother had said my mother went back because she had problems living here. I told her what Annie said. She said she knew—"

"I told him I knew about the story in the hospital," Mrs. Winkel interjected. She would put the right face on the narrative. "The story didn't matter. Nobody could prove a thing. But it was too bad this girl came along that guessed some of it. And then she married Matty."

"And never knew her husband was also a ghost," I said. It seemed almost unbelievable, but Annie had surely not wandered through cemeteries, looking for names to match with living men. "Have you seen your mother since, Val?"

"Once. I took a trip abroad after Annie told me. I asked my mother for the truth because I wanted to know it for myself. What she said didn't convince me. I never saw her again."

"Did Matty know what Annie had found out about you?"

"I never told him. I didn't think Annie'd ever talk to him about it, and I thought the less said, the better off we all were."

"So Matty never knew you had a life insurance policy for a million dollars with him as the beneficiary."

"He never knew. That was between Annie and me."

I looked down at my notebook. There were a few unanswered questions, but I didn't think Val or his grandmother could help me with them. "I think that's about it," I said. "What are you planning to do now?"

"I think I'll have to turn myself in. I've been wrestling with this for three months. I owe it to Jake, and I owe it to Carlotta."

"You owe it to yourself, Val," I said. "I'm sure you'll be vindicated."

He didn't look very sure himself, and his grandmother started to put up an argument against his returning to the States. But he went upstairs, packed the small number of clothes he had bought since his arrival in February, and came back down. He was ready to do it.

26

The departure from the little house in Canada left all of us in tears. Despite my harsh feelings about Val's grandmother, I recognized that the woman had devoted her life to her three grandsons, that she had accepted them in their times of need, ministered to them, and asked for nothing in return. I could scarcely imagine the pain she felt at the death of the other two grandsons.

She was tough till the last second, the first tears materializing as Val let her go at the front door. A big woman, she seemed almost small in his arms. We walked down the path to the street, then around the corner to the car. Carlotta drove and I sat in the back, thinking it all over.

On the trip home, Val said he had taken his grandmother to Toronto the previous week. He had looked for a job there, feeling the time had come to venture out of the house and make a new life for himself. The young girl who had opened the door for us had been exactly what she claimed to be, a neighbor who was cat-sitting. She had never seen Val and had been evasive because she thought our questions were strange.

It was much too late that night to call Detective Murdock, but I reached him first thing in the morning.

"Anything interesting to tell me?" he asked.

"A number of things. One, I have a witness you will want to talk to, and two, I know who killed Matty Franklin."

"OK, Ms. Bennett," he said in a humoring tone of voice. "When can I see your witness?"

"As soon as you come to Mrs. Krassky's house. We'll be waiting for you."

He promised to be there within the hour, and he was as good as his word. The look on his face when I introduced Valentine Krassky was worth the wait.

Carlotta and I sat in the adjoining family room where we could hear the interrogation, such as it was, but we couldn't see the men's faces. Carlotta looked spellbound, her face toward the open door to the living room, while I sat with my back to it. All the questions had to do with the events of February fourteenth and the weeks that had followed. Val said he had stayed with "friends" in Canada, and Murdock didn't challenge that or ask for any elaboration. He was interested in finding a killer, and the peripheral facts, the ones that had led me to Val, were of no interest to him.

Finally it sounded as though the interview was coming to an end. Murdock came into the family room and nodded rather gallantly at both of us. "Ms. Bennett, I owe you a very big thank-you."

"You're more than welcome, Detective. I'd like to make a suggestion before you leave. Val isn't sure what happened to the murder weapon. On the chance that Mrs. Franklin may have carried it home with her, I'd like to suggest you get a warrant and search her house. I also think it might be useful to take some photos she has in her album. You'll see that she's wearing the red scarf, not her husband."

"It was my understanding that the scarf was his."

"It was given to him as a Christmas present, but when did that ever stop a wife from 'borrowing' something of her husband's?"

He smiled. "You mean like my favorite black cashmere sweater that I haven't worn since two days after my birthday because my wife preempted it?"

"Just like that."

"What was it about the scarf that got you digging?"

"Several things. The fact that it just lay on the ice, that it wasn't soaked or scrunched up. If Matty or Clark had been using it to hoist themselves out of the water and failed, the scarf would most likely have gone down with them. If that's your lifeline, you hang onto it forever. But it wasn't. It was just pulled off someone, accidentally. When Val described what had happened out there, I understood how. But I was already curious about that scarf. It just didn't seem right that it was lying so pristinely on the ice. Then, when I picked Mrs. Krassky up yesterday to take her to the airport, she was wearing a beautiful wool shirt of her husband's. That stuck with me. Mrs. Franklin showed me some photos yesterday afternoon, and then I saw who wore the scarf, and I guessed she had been there that night." I didn't add what I'd learned about where Annie came from and what she knew.

"I'll get that warrant."

"Detective Murdock, I'd really like to be there when you talk to Annie Franklin."

He thought a moment. "I think that can be arranged. I owe you one for your help. Stay by the phone."

I promised I would.

* * *

I went back upstairs and stuffed back in my bag the few things I had unpacked. It was winding down, my last case, and I could feel the letdown settle in. When I went back downstairs I could hear the muffled voices of my hosts, unintelligible questions and answers, an occasional laugh, as they worked their way through the three months they had lived separately.

"Chris? Come join us for a cup of tea."

I walked into the breakfast room where they sat at the round table, tea and newspapers scattered between them. "Maybe a glass of milk," I said, passing into the kitchen to find it for myself. I poured myself a glass and carried it to the table. "Have you talked to Jake yet?"

"First thing this morning."

"I bet he's happy."

"Almost as happy as I am."

"Tell me, you must have thought a lot about Carlotta. Did you have any idea what you would do?"

"I knew I'd contact her, but I wasn't sure when. I felt I should be working before I got in touch. I spent the first few weeks in a kind of haze. I had all these assets, but they were all in my name only. If I tried to use them, I'd blow my cover. I didn't know what to do. Finally I decided I just had to start over. It left Jake in a difficult position, but I was afraid if I came forward I'd face a murder charge and no one would believe Annie was guilty. I just spent every day trying to work out a way of getting free of what had happened."

"I know you were helping out your grandmother and paying Annie when she demanded it. Did you ever give money to Clark and his family?"

"He wouldn't take it; I tried. I felt I was the senior member of the group and I had to look out for the others.

I made enough that I could afford to. Annie came to me a lot for handouts, but when I tried to even things out and give something to Clark, he wouldn't hear of it. Clark was a very straight arrow, younger than his official age, a guy who just wanted to do his thing and be with his family. He was in the wrong place at the wrong time on Valentine's Day. I guess we all were."

"And his mother and Matty's was long dead."

"As long as I can remember."

About one o'clock Detective Murdock called. He and a sheriff's deputy were on their way to the Franklin house. I could meet them there.

I went alone. Annie wasn't home. Murdock found a key in a potted plant near the side door, and I followed them into the house. I kept my hands to myself, but showed Murdock where the photo albums were. He collected several pictures that showed Annie wearing the red scarf, then he and the deputy systematically looked for the missing gun while I watched them work. I wanted them to find that gun. Val's story was believable, and the pictures with the red scarf were nice to look at, but there's nothing like a weapon to seal the fate of a shooter.

It wasn't mixed in with Matty's hunting guns. It wasn't in the basement where Matty kept his tools and garden equipment. It wasn't in the garage or in the car or in any of the drawers in the large family room.

Finally I followed the men up to the second floor to Annie's beautiful bedroom. There was no gun in either of the night tables, or in any of her dresser drawers. It wasn't in the closet, and there was no obvious place in the bathroom that it could have been hidden.

I looked around the room. "Did you try Matty's chest?" I asked.

"Just about to," the deputy said. "You'd think if she kept a gun, she'd have it next to the bed where she could reach for it."

"Maybe it wasn't for protection," I said.

They looked at me, but I added nothing. Maybe Annie had planned this for years, or at least thought about it. Maybe she had a gun so she could kill Val when the time was right, and for no other reason.

They started with the top of the chest of drawers. Matty's clothes were still in there, as though he might return tonight and need a fresh pair of socks and a clean set of underwear. They went slowly down, drawer by drawer. I looked at my watch, knowing that Annie would have to return soon, that her children were getting out of school, that an arrest could hardly stick if it were her word against his.

"Got something." It was Murdock's voice. He was down on his knees at the lowest drawer. He pulled at something, then brought out an object covered with a man's old shirt. Carefully unwrapping it, he held it out for us to see. It was a handgun.

Annie was like a mad cat. She stormed into the house just as we were about to go outside and wait for her. The warrant made no difference; Murdock's courtesy counted for nothing.

"How dare you!" she shouted. "What are you doing in my house?"

"We're executing a legal search warrant, Mrs. Franklin," Murdock said.

"Get out of here. I forbid you to touch anything in here."

"We're done with our search, ma'am. I'm going to have to advise you of your rights."

"My rights? What do my rights have to do with anything?"

"I'm arresting you for the murder of Matthew Franklin."

She collected her thoughts for a moment, her gaze touching each of us. "I didn't do it," she said. "He did it, Val. He hated Matty. Val wanted me. That's what this was about."

"I don't think so, Mrs. Franklin. We've found the gun."

Her eyes opened wide. "I had to protect myself from him," she said desperately. "He was an imposter. His mother killed a child in Connecticut and gave Val the boy's name."

"Mrs. Franklin, you have the right to remain silent. You have the—"

"I'm innocent, you have to believe me. I don't know anything about a gun. He's alive, you know. He shot my husband and he got away. He's probably in Europe now."

"He's alive, all right," Murdock said. "I took a statement from him this morning. If you promise not to make a fuss, ma'am, I won't put the cuffs on till we're in the car."

Her mouth shook. "My children," she whispered.

"I'll stay here and wait for them," I said. "Let her get a toothbrush, Detective."

"You bet."

They went upstairs together, and I sat down to think about what I would be doing with the rest of my life.

27

Annie's last words to me would sting in my memory. After coming down the stairs with a small duffel bag, she came over to me. "It wasn't supposed to happen that way," she said. "Val was supposed to go down with the first shot, and I was supposed to go home. Rich. Val doesn't really exist, you know. He's just a shadow."

"OK, Mrs. Franklin," Detective Murdock said. "This way." He turned back to me. "I'll have the social services people pick up the children. You know if she has any family around here?"

"Greenwich, Connecticut, I think. You'll have to ask her. I don't know her maiden name."

I watched the car leave. Several neighbors, all women and children, stood on the quiet street, talking and watching. It was a moment they would never forget, as I would also remember it.

Then, down the street, I saw the first of Matty and Annie's children skipping toward home.

Murdock called me at Carlotta's as I was getting ready to leave for the airport. The social services people had arrived not long after the children had come home.

"The gun is registered to Winston Hargrave, Mrs. Franklin's older brother."

"Is it the murder weapon?"

"We won't know for a while but it's the right caliber. I'll let you know."

"Thank you."

"Well, it's you that deserves the thanks. Maybe we can have a nice long telephone conversation later this week, and you can tell me how you found my man."

"I'll be glad to, Detective. Call any time. I'm on my way home now."

"Take a nice long rest. You deserve it."

Carlotta drove me to the airport while Val went to visit Jake Halpern.

"You must have a lot of catching up to do," I said as we headed towards Buffalo.

"I was wrong about some things, Chris. About whether Val would make that awful trek across the lake. You're right that you never know another human being as well as you know yourself. But I was right about what's important. I've never loved anyone in my life as much as I love Val. And he feels the same way about me. We're as solid as the day he gave me the ring." She moved her hand, and the red stone picked up the light and flashed.

"Have you talked about who he is, and what he remembers of his early childhood?"

"He's the man I married. He's the man who's Jake Halpern's partner. He's the man I fell in love with that weekend I went skiing all those years ago. None of the rest matters. We'll get a good lawyer and straighten out the details. But that's all they are, details. I have my husband back, Chris. I've never been happier."

I smiled. "Me, too."

"And I hope you'll let me know the minute the baby comes. I want him to know he has an aunt in Buffalo who's there whenever he needs me."

"That's very kind of you."

She looked at the ring again and smiled, a very private smile. She was a happy woman.

The addition seemed to grow by the day. It was only yesterday afternoon that I had seen it last, and now it was subtly different. I went upstairs and looked through the connecting opening. The subflooring was there, the insulation, the hole in the wall where the air conditioner I had allowed myself to be talked into would be installed. It was a beautiful room, and the adjoining bathroom, with its linen closet and handsome stall shower, was more luxury than I had ever imagined would be ours.

I called Melanie and told her I was home for good. We chatted happily, and then I sat down with yesterday's newspaper. I didn't read much. I had brought my last case to an end, a successful end, but an end nevertheless. Now I would drink my milk, tend my garden, do my exercise, perhaps do some work for Arnold Gold, whom I missed very much. In the fall I would teach. Then I would give birth, and I would see. But a most enjoyable part of my life had just come to a close.

Jack came home at his usual late hour, and I told him how it had ended.

"Did you tell Murdock about the possible homicide in Connecticut?"

"I didn't. You and I will have to talk about it first. I don't know if there's enough solid information to build a case. And maybe there isn't any case. Maybe the little boy died, and the woman got scared and ran."

"But you got Val and his wife back together again."

"They're back. They're very nice people, Jack. I'm glad it's worked out for them."

"Oh, hey. I forgot to tell you. Remember your mother's old friend Elsie Rivers?"

"Sure."

"She called last night, and I didn't have a piece of paper so I forgot to write it down. I hope you don't mind. She was so sweet and asked so many questions, I let the cat out of the bag. I told her we're expecting."

"That's OK, Jack. I bet she's pleased."

"Pleased is an understatement. She's ecstatic. It's like this is her own grandchild. She reminded me that her own kids are far away, that she and your mom were as close as two peas in a pod, that she can't wait to hold this baby."

"She's very sweet."

"It goes on. If you want to teach, you just drop the baby off and she'll take care of it. If you want to take a vacation, she has a room the baby can stay in and a crib all set up. If you want to go into the city— What are you grinning at?"

"I never thought of Elsie," I said. "You know what? Maybe the murder on the lake wasn't my last case, after all."

Even after leaving the cloistered world
of St. Stephen's Convent for suburban
New York State, Christine Bennett
still finds time to celebrate the holy days.

Unfortunately, in the secular world
the holidays seem to end in murder—
and it's up to this ex-nun
to discover who commits
these unholy acts.

LEE HARRIS

The Christine Bennett Mysteries

Look for these Christine Bennett mysteries by

LEE HARRIS

in your local bookstore.
Published by Fawcett Books.